CRIMINAL CHRISTMAS COMPLETE COLLECTION

CONNOR WHITELEY

No part of this book may be reproduced in any form or by any electronic or mechanical means. Including information storage, and retrieval systems, without written permission from the author except for the use of brief quotations in a book review.

This book is NOT legal, professional, medical, financial or any type of official advice.

Any questions about the book, rights licensing, or to contact the author, please email connorwhiteley@connorwhiteley.net

Copyright © 2023 CONNOR WHITELEY

All rights reserved.

DEDICATION
Thank you to all my readers without you I couldn't do what I love.

INTRODUCTION

If you ask anyone about what fiction genres naturally go with the holiday season, you will most probably hear a lot of romances, fantasy and maybe a few other subgenres. But you will very rarely hear people expecting to read mystery and crime stories during the holiday season.

However I couldn't disagree more because the mystery genre perfectly fits the holiday season. It is the perfect contrast to all the goodie-tooshie rubbish that dominates the season with all the gift giving, carols and the rest of the happy stuff.

So in this mystery and crime collection based on the Holiday Extravaganza 2022 (with the introductions for each short story included), I wanted to write a bunch of mysteries and crime stories that showcased the darker and less innocent side of the holiday season.

The vast majority of the stories are all perfectly light, but that doesn't stop the collection showing the wide range of the mystery genre. From women sleuths and private eyes investigating crimes throughout the month, to criminals wanting to steal from others to a son needing to protect his siblings. Even if it means killing his mother.

Definitely keep reading, lock the doors and prepare yourself for the gripping, unputdownable full force of holiday mystery stories that will keep you reading late into the night.

You are seriously in for a great treat!

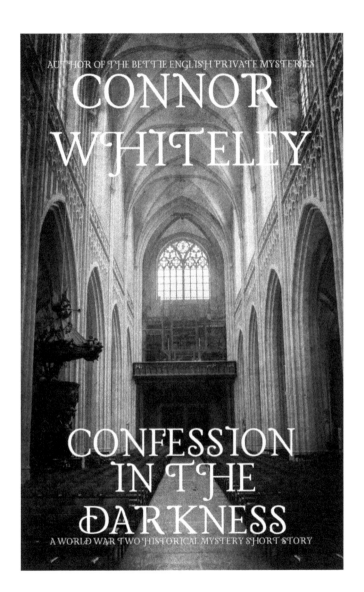

INTRODUCTION
Mood/ Genre: Light Historical Fiction Spy Story

Whilst this is the first story you're officially seeing in the Holiday Extravaganza, this actually wasn't meant to be in the Extravaganza because the original story, that will kick off next year's Extravaganza now, got called away so I needed a replacement.

And there really is absolutely no better way to kick of this sensational Holiday Extravaganza by looking deep in the darkest days of World War Two at a very brave woman spy in this brilliant, relatable and enthralling short story that is most certainly different from the types of Holiday stories you might have been expecting.

The story doesn't exactly set the tone of the Extravaganza per se, but you will absolutely love it and even if you don't traditionally enjoy historical fiction, this story might have the power to change your mind.

Enjoy!

CONFESSION IN THE DARKNESS
27th December 1943
St Paul's Cathedral, London, England

The arid aroma of burning petrol, smoke and smouldering buildings, leaving the taste of burnt food on her tongue, gently filtered through into St Paul's cathedral as French Resistance Leader Marie-Madeline Hall sat on one of the massive cold wooden pews in a row of them that seemed to stretch on endlessly, and the dark, almost black wood of the pews seemed like such a stunning, but stark, contrast against the gently shining gold, silver and bronze of the altar up ahead.

Marie-Madeline had been in England for a good few months now after being flown out of France at the insistence of MI6, the British Spy agency, and her own closest lieutenants, and even now she still found St Paul's to be an impressive reminder of the power of faith in the darkest of hours.

The immense marble altar was a beautiful reminder of humanity's ability to build and live and worship peacefully without the need to wage a global war against each other, and the massive golden statues and decorative details honouring Christ and many more amazing figures of the bible was another beautiful reminder that Marie-Madeline really needed to savour for the times ahead.

It might have been late in the evening with the only light daring to illuminate St Paul's were a few carefully placed candles that burnt slowly like beacons of hope in the ever-growing darkness that was the war, Marie-Madeline had still been expecting a few more worshippers to honour the cathedral with their presence, especially so close after the Lord Jesus Christ's birthday, the very best of celebrations indeed.

But only Marie-Madeline and another five people were sitting in the pews, and the other five people were so far away sitting on other rows upon rows of pews that she couldn't even really see them clearly. They were mostly women but that was to be expected given the dire state of the war, and Marie-Madeline just wished she had some comfort for them.

She didn't.

Those women were probably here for the exact same reason she was, because she wanted guidance to relax some of her fears about going back to France, her home, the country she loved, and the country she just wanted, needed to be free.

Marie-Madeline was deadly certain that she wanted to go back to France, it was in her blood after all and she never wanted to leave in the first place, but that was before most of her network had fallen, her resources had been destroyed and some of her best friends in the entire world had been captured, and were probably dead now.

Marie-Madeline smiled to herself for a moment because that was exactly why she had to go back to France, because it needed her and Marie-Madeline needed France to be free, and if there was any chance that her friends were still alive then she absolutely had to stop the war and get them back.

No matter the cost.

The sound of footsteps, people muttering prays and a person coughing echoed around the cathedral as Marie-Madeline focused on a very tall man in the black clothes of a priest walk past, and he looked at her and bowed her head.

"Do you need anything dear child?" the Priest asked.

Marie-Madeline wanted to scream and shout *yes* to that question and tell him all of her fears and worries and concerns about returning to France after so long, but if she had learnt anything about being a female leader of a resistance group and operating in a man's world, it was that calmness was a girl's best friend.

"Are you free for confession padre?" Marie-Madeline asked.

The Priest smiled and gestured her to follow him.

Marie-Madeline felt her stomach twist into a painful knot because this was the first time she was allowing herself to realise just how nervous she was about returning to France.

And she had forbidden herself her processing these emotions for so long she was just scared of what she would say and she what she was going to do about the future.

Because Marie-Madeline just knew what happened tonight could decide the fate of the war.

***

27th December 1943

St Paul's Cathedral, London, England

Even before the war, Marie-Madeline had never really liked confessional booths, and this one might have been in thee St Paul's but it was still just as cramped and small and horrible as all the other booths she had been in over her life travelling the world, but still trying to keep her faith as strong as she possibly could.

Marie-Madeline sat on a very uncomfortable chair in the dark brown confessional booth, and the chair was a little silly in its own right because the "pillow" on it was nothing more than a thin piece of cloth, not exactly comfortable but she wasn't here for comfort, she was here for guidance from God.

The confessional booth wasn't even large enough for Marie-Madeline to stretch her arms out in and the little booth smelt of sweat, dried tears and something musky that Marie-Madeline couldn't identify. She had little doubt the priest had tried to cover up the smell with a faint burning of incense but that did little in reality.

The only advantage of the smell was that Marie-Madeline no longer had to breathe in the horrible aromas of the bombings and attacks on London like she did in the main area of the cathedral.

Marie-Madeline heard someone shuffle around in the booth next to her and moments later, a small panel opened revealing the Priest through a golden metal grate.

And then for the first time Marie-Madeline really focused on the priest, and he was a rather attractive man considering his advanced age, grey hair and his war-hardened face.

Marie-Madeline would have been surprised if the man hadn't fought in the 1914-18 war and now he was just tired of the world fighting itself all over again, Marie-Madeline could really, really understand that.

"Forgive me father for I have sinned, it has been seven days since my last confession," Marie-Madeline said.

"Child of God," the Priest said, "this is a time of war and God testing us, he will forgive you fighting the Devil's influence,"

Marie-Madeline was impressed that the priest seemed to know exactly who she was and what she did. Granted that was hardly surprising given how many of the UK's top politicians, spies and other assets came here, Marie-Madeline would have been surprised if one of them hadn't mentioned her or at least her spy network, considering it was the largest in

France.

"God sees all dear Child, what is it that you fear,"

Marie-Madeline didn't want to answer the question, she didn't want to admit to God that she was weaker than others believed her to be, she wasn't sure she could handle the challenges he would throw at her and she really wasn't sure she could undo the Enemy's work in God's divine land.

But she couldn't not answer God.

"I am meant to return to France soon but, I am unsure if I am stronger enough to lead my network after so long. I am not even sure much of it survives," Marie-Madeline said.

The Priest nodded. "God gives us challenges to face but only those that he knows we can face. To doubt the His plan to is to doubt God, and that only leads to damnation dear child,"

Marie-Madeline wanted to disagree, surely doubt was good from time to time. Her doubting her plans and revisiting them and improving her plans had saved her and her network more times than she cared to count, far more times than this priest of all people could possibly understand being locked away in the safety of England for so long.

"You doubt His Plan?" the Priest asked.

Marie-Madeline nodded. "God gives me strength and I don't know how but I know guides my actions but, I don't know how to return to France and win the war for Him,"

Marie-Madeline wasn't exactly sure if she was

fighting the war for God per se, but given how she was inside a confessional booth, she knew she just needed to keep sounding zealous enough and maybe the priest would give her a piece of information that was actually useful.

"What are you most scared of dear Child of God?"

Marie-Madeline smiled because ever since the war first started she had only ever had a single fear. Or a range of fears that boiled down to a single deadly point.

"Being captured," Marie-Madeline said.

The Priest nodded fiercely and maybe if she had met him in a "pub" as the English called it, she might have asked what had happened to him in the 1914-18 war, because she had seen the look of horror veterans had all too many times in recent months and that was the exact look the Priest had now.

"God has a plan," the Priest said. "I was captured in the battle of the Somme decades ago, and the Germans tortured, beat and did worse to me. I kept my faith, I kept believing in Him and he rewarded me because he guided the allies to my position and I was freed,"

As much as Marie-Madeline wanted to believe the priest, she just couldn't help but think that maybe God had nothing to do with any of this war and the heroic deeds of it.

Maybe God was just a mythical piece of faith that humans used to keep themselves calm and maybe

God wasn't real in the slightest.

"I truly fear His judgement," Marie-Madeline said as she took out two white cyanide tablets that a British spy friend of hers had given her recently just in case.

Marie-Madeline knew that it was logical to want to die instead of falling into enemy hands. Especially as she knew so much about British and French resistance activity, she knew codes and encryptions and the locations of battlegroups.

Marie-Madeline was far too important to fall into enemy hands so surely killing herself was the best way to serve the war effort if it ever came to that.

But Marie-Madeline just couldn't get over the fact that if she killed herself then she was dishonouring God as she was one of his creations and she might go to hell for what seemed like a great idea at the time.

The Priest slowly nodded. "I see your problem dear child of God but know that this is not about dishonouring God it is about something else entirely,"

Marie-Madeline leant closely to the golden metal grate and she really hoped that this was the amazing piece of information that she had been waiting for.

"If you deny the enemy information against the forces of good and people that want to use God's light as a beacon of hope against the darkness. Then this is not dishonouring God, it is simply preventing the enemy and God would forgive you. Jesus sacrificed himself for humanity almost two thousand years ago and now we must all aspire to be as great as he was,"

Marie-Madeline instantly bowed her head slightly as what the priest was saying felt so true, right and real.

And what really surprised her was that Marie-Madeline felt something almost click inside her, like all of her past worries and concerns and fears were disappearing because she knew that God was important, right and he would guide her actions in helping the allies win the war.

No matter how impossible it seemed.

"Thank you padre," Marie-Madeline said.

"May the Lord watch over you," the Priest said as he closed the panel and the golden metal grate disappeared behind a small piece of dark brown wood.

Marie-Madeline sat in the confessional booth for a few more moments and couldn't believe how amazing and light and brilliant she felt, and it was only now that Marie-Madeline was realising how worried she had been earlier.

Marie-Madeline stood up and prepared to leave the confessional booth as a brand new woman, because she had God on her side, and now she was really looking forward to traveling back to France, rebuilding her resistance network and doing exactly what she had been doing so brilliantly for the past four years.

Making sure the British had the best intelligence

they could to win the war.

Marie-Madeline opened the wooden door of the confessional booth, lit a candle for all her fallen agents at the altar a few metres away and she simply left St Paul's cathedral descending into the darkness of a busy London street.

Because she had a lot of work to do and she couldn't believe how excited she was to get back to it all, and win her country's freedom once and for all.

PROTECTING CHRISTMAS

A HOLIDAY MYSTERY CRIME SHORT STORY

CONNOR WHITELEY

AUTHOR OF BETTIE ENGLISH PRIVATE EYE MYSTERIES

INTRODUCTION
Mood/ Genre: Light Crime

If you thought you were only going to get wonderfully light goody-two-shoe stories from me then I hate (not) to tell you, you are sadly mistaken.

But don't worry because today we have a great light crime short story as it is National Package Protection Day.

When I first heard of this made-up holiday, my mind immediately went to two different places on the mystery fiction spectrum. I was tempted to write a Bettie Private Eye short story set today, but then I realised I ready had a few of them lined up for the Holiday Extravaganza.

Thankfully my mind went somewhere else too, it went to the criminal side. Because surely the packages need to be protected from something?

Cue criminals!

But our next story is filled with twists and surprises, so if you think this is your normal theft

short story, think again!
Enjoy!

PROTECTING CHRISTMAS

National Parcel Protection Day (in the US at least) had to be the greatest of Holidays to Jessica, it was a day basically begging for crime to be committed, parcels stolen and their protectors in tears over their failures.

And Jessica was only too happy to oblige.

Jessica wasn't a bad person, she didn't steal for herself, she didn't steal for thrills or any of those so-called excuses, she stole for the good of others.

That reason was a simple excuse according to many of her friends but Jessica loved the holiday season and National Parcel Protection Day most of all, it was her way of giving back.

As Jessica stood in the wonderful little street with small houses packed together with a (rather pathetic) little road separating them, Jessica felt the excitement filling her as she prepared for her first steal of the day.

The air smelt wonderfully of warming Christmas spices, one of the houses were probably baking some mince pies, a little early but each to their own, and Jessica loved the sound of the children singing (badly) at school a few blocks away.

Jessica wasn't sure if she liked the neighbourhood or houses along the street too much. Sure they had Christmas decorations, lights and wreaths hanging all over them. But there was something strange about them, they were all the same, identical and not in a beautiful way.

The bitter cold was another reason Jessica didn't like the neighbourhood, every neighbourhood in England had a certain (extremely varying) degree of charm to it and even the houses that were meant to look alike had their own faults and aspects of character to it.

These houses did not.

If Jessica was to guess, she might have believed some American developer had created this street or something but she didn't know. And she most certainly didn't want to find out. This street felt weird.

The wonderfully spice scented air got stronger and Jessica licked her lips as she imagined their amazing fruity, spicy taste in her mouth. Maybe she would have to steal some for herself.

Jessica hated that idea. That was flat out wrong, stealing for oneself was never good and Jessica had learnt that first hand as a child.

As a homeless child living, eating and stealing on the streets, she had to get food somehow but she stole from the wrong baker one day, and ended by getting beaten within an inch of her life because of it.

When she recovered, got a job a few years later and learnt that her true family had died in a car crash and left her some money, Jessica vowed to help those on the streets like no one had ever done for her.

The sound of the children singing started to die down as the howl of the bitter wind grew. That was probably the worse thing about the streets, their cold unloving nature. Maybe she would buy some thick coats for the homeless with the money she got from today's theft.

The sound of a large white van driving slowly down the street made Jessica stare at it. Jessica wasn't a fan of white vans, they reminded her too much of scary child kidnapping films and there was something about the speed of the van.

The van shouldn't have been driving that slowly, the entire street was perfectly clean of cars, so the van was hardly going to bump into anything.

Jessica stepped back a little and focused on the drivers. There was one man wearing a black tracksuit and a black cap covering most of his face, and a tall woman was wearing a long black coat.

But what Jessica didn't like was how they were looking each house up and down and around.

That look was all too familiar to Jessica, she had given the entire road those looks twice today already. She had calculated from a bit of research that the post people always come at 12 o'clock on this road like clockwork.

It was almost time and all the houses in the road were empty.

Jessica wasn't sure what the people in the van were doing but she didn't like it. She wanted to go over there, pound on the window and get them to go. This was her road to steal from and at least she was going to give her stolen items to a good cause.

These people weren't, Jessica had run into these sorts of people before. White van drivers that were thieves were never good people to get involved with.

If she could just get one parcel without those people seeing her, then she could get something for the homeless people.

The sound of the van doors slamming shut made Jessica's eyes widen as she saw the man and woman leant against the van and stare at her.

Jessica didn't know what to do. She could run, but she didn't want to be chased.

"You wanna parcel?" the man asked.

Jessica was surprised by his deep, disease ridden voice. He definitely wasn't the healthiest man she had ever met, but there was something creepy about him. The way he stared at her and bit his lip.

"Ah come on Luv," the man said, gesturing her to come close.

Jessica wasn't sure why they were here. If the man and woman had been here for parcels then they should have waited in the van, seen the post people leave the parcels and then steal them.

But they wanted Jessica to come closer to them.

She didn't like this one bit.

"I've got some presents in my van ya can have," the man said.

Jessica's mouth dropped. This man and woman were foul people, they wanted to kidnap her. Jessica was shocked. How dare they come to this street, on her favourite National Day and try to pull a stunt like this.

The sound of children cheering echoed around the neighbour from the school.

"Leave!" Jessica shouted.

She wasn't going to let them kidnap a child if that was their plan, if the local school was finishing earlier today then Jessica was never going to let one of the children anywhere near these people.

Jessica had almost been stolen herself on the streets before, she was never ever going to let another child experience that!

"We ain't doing anything wrong. We just waiting outside out van," the woman said.

Jessica sneered at them both. "What's your plan then? Steal a few children. Get their parents to pay you. Then have a merry Christmas,"

The man and woman smiled at each other.

"What is it to ya?" the man asked.

"I will not let you steal children on my day!"

The man laughed. "Ya Day? What are ya the Queen?"

Queen Jessica, it did have a nice ring to it. But as much as Jessica loved that idea, she had to try to do something today of all days. The holiday was meant to be about Protection after all.

"Go now or I *will* call the police," Jessica said.

The man mockingly cried. "Ya really think ta police will show up for two peeps leaning against a van,"

Jessica wanted to protest but that was a harsh truth about the world they lived in. Years of cut backs, politics and everything had left all public services decimated to varying degrees, the police was no less affected than any other public service.

After spending about ten years as a police call handler Jessica remembered that all too well.

"Tell ya what luv. Leave. We let you live," the man said.

Jessica shook her head. "I am not leaving you two alone,"

"Come on, you must have some fam. Ready want 'em to receive your ransom?" the woman said.

Jessica was glad she didn't have any still alive. She hated her true family for abandoning her and when they died it was almost joyous to her. But how dare these idiots threaten her, they were going to be in for a hell of a surprise. She had lived on the streets long enough to learn how to defend herself.

The amazing smell of warm mince pies made Jessica realise there had to be someone at home in one of the houses, maybe if she was loud enough they would check on the situation.

But what would it look like?

She wasn't sure. All it probably looked like were two strange people leaning against a van and a crazy woman who clearly wasn't from the neighbourhood shouting at them.

"My family wouldn't pay for pay anyway," Jessica said.

The man grabbed his genitals. "I would luv,"

That was the final straw, Jessica had to do something. This man was disgusting and it was even more disgusting that this lady friend (girlfriend, wife, mistress?) wasn't saying anything.

Then Jessica remembered how cruel both men and women can be to homeless children on the street.

Jessica looked at her watch. It was a few minutes to twelve. The post people would be here soon, maybe that could save her and the children.

"You need to go now!" Jessica shouted, tapping her watch.

The man grinned. "Ya think ta postman is gonna stop us. We'll just gut him, like we will ya!"

The man whipped out a knife.

The woman did the same.

Jessica froze.

They both ran at her.

Her street training kicked in.

The man swung.

Jessica ducked.

Slamming her fists into his jaw.

He moaned.

Jessica kicked the woman in the chest.

She screamed.

The man swung again.

Quickly.

There were too many strikes coming.

Jessica ducked.

She rolled.

She jumped up.

Smashing her fists into the man's spine.

Something cracked.

The woman swung.

Jessica punched her.

The knife almost cutting her.

The woman jumped forward.

Knocking Jessica to the ground.

The knife sliced her.

The woman attacked again.

Thrusting the knife into Jessica's chest.

She screamed.

Jessica grabbed the woman's hands.

Forcing the knife to remain in her.

The woman looked scared.

Jessica headbutted her.

She let go of the knife.

Jessica whacked the woman.

She fell to the ground.

Jessica stomped on her head.

The man got up.

Jessica kicked him in the head.

Jessica frowned at the man and woman on the ground with blood on their face and a wave of discomfort washed over Jessica as she feared they were dead. She never wanted to kill them.

Jessica checked their pulses.

To her relief both the man and the woman were unconscious and not dead. A very small part of her wanted them dead, at least that way they wouldn't be able to hurt any more children ever again.

But the truth for Jessica was she wasn't a killer. Even during her darkest days on the streets, she never hurt anyone who didn't deserve it.

She bit her lip as a wave of pain from the stab wound washed over her. Jessica pressed the wound gently and she was relieved that it wasn't bleeding, it wasn't a bad cut and at least she would still be around to help the homeless.

The sound of police sirens in the distance was almost angelic to Jessica as that had to be a sign that the children would be safe and these two would be sent to prison. At least she had somehow honoured her favourite National Day, whilst she didn't have any presents for the homeless people today, at least she had protected the innocent from these idiots.

And that was a good day in her books.

The sound of the police sirens were getting closer so Jessica went up to the back of the white van, kicked the lock and opened it for the police.

Jessica was shocked at all the rope, candies and comic books that the two creeps had both for the children. She was more than glad she had stopped them now and at least the police could clearly see that the man and woman were the bad guys, and not her.

As Jessica walked off into the distance leaving the police to find the man, woman and the incriminating white van, Jessica was filled with delight that her National Parcel Day had gone so perfectly.

She was going to remember this for a long, long time.

INTRODUCTION

Genre/Mood: Warming Amateur Sleuth Mystery

All over the world, food plays a central part in the holiday season and it always plays a major part in all religious events. Christmas is no different, because at least in the UK, there is a rather large emphasis played on the famous Christmas cake.

But what if your Christmas Cake gets stolen?

In most families, and mine was no different, there was a grandmother who specialises in making them and making sure all the family members get to try some, and my muse loved that holiday tradition.

So in early 2021, I was writing a set of amateur sleuth short stories about Jane Smith a retired woman in a small village, and suddenly her Christmas cake was stolen.

Expect a warming wonderful story about love, family and friendship that is just perfect for the next story in the Holiday Extravaganza!

Enjoy!

CRIMINAL CHRISTMAS COMPLETE COLLECTION

CHRISTMAS THIEF

Amateur Sleuth Jane Smith just loved Christmas more than any other time of the year (maybe except for her children's birthdays), there was so much amazing magic about Christmas, and of course Jane loved the food, presents and family too.

Ever since she had been a kid, Jane had always been obsessed with Christmas, it was fun, exciting and she loved eating her way through the season, and then when she had kids, her love for the season only grew in intensity.

Every year Jane would make sure her kids got the best Christmas they possibly could, and even with the kids leaving home and returning to Jane's small village in the south of England with their families for Christmas, she still tried her hardest to make it rememberable.

As Jane placed the freshly made Christmas cake on the wooden worktop of her kitchen, Jane took deep wonderful breaths of the cake's amazing aroma that made the house smell of rich fruits, sugar and more than enough alcohol to knock out a horse.

Jane just admired the cakes great brown colour, rich fruit and everything about the cake was just wonderful. To Jane this was the start of the holiday season, making the cake in early December was just perfect and it showed her that she needed to start getting her bum in gear about the rest of it.

Jane listened to the wonderful quiet singing in the background of Christmas songs that she had playing on her record player, she had tried to download something called *mp3s* before, but they never sounded as good as real records.

As Jane's kitchen started to fill up with steam, she went over to one of the windows that lined a wall of the kitchen and she popped it open. When the cold breeze rushed past her, Jane realised how hot it was in the kitchen, and that made her smile as that was always a part of Christmas.

Christmas had to be cold for Jane.

When her two kids were really young, her and her husband had taken them to America for Christmas, but everyone had hated it because Christmas was so over the top in America, and it was so hot. Christmas wasn't about money or heat to Jane, it was about love, food and family, some points that trip completely failed on.

A knock at the front door made Jane hiss as she made sure her wonderful Christmas cake was perfectly level on the worktop, she wasn't going to have hours of work (and cooking fun) drop onto the floor if she could help it.

Jane went through her house, into the little hallway and opened her front door to see her best friend standing there in the freezing cold, shaking.

"Come in Marg,"

"Thanks Pet," Marg said as she walked in and Jane led her out into the kitchen.

Jane popped on the kettle and pointed to a small round table that she had tucked away into the corner of the kitchen and Marg pulled out one of the chairs underneath and sat down.

But the kitchen was a lot colder than she remembered, she made a mental note to shut the window in a moment.

Jane had to admit she hadn't been expecting her best friend today, she had definitely hadn't expected her to walk from the other side of the village in the freezing cold to see her. Jane didn't know whether to be happy or concerned.

"Nice cake Pet,"

"Thanks," Jane said, as she finished making the tea and bought it over to Marg, "Why you here? Wasn't expecting you today,"

"Yea Pet. I just wanna…" Marg said.

Jane stared at her best friend out of concern more than anything because Marg never just trailed off, but then Jane realised Marg wasn't staring at her, she was staring past her at the cake.

Jane turned around and gasped when she saw

half the Christmas Cake had been… cut away and was gone. Someone had stolen her legendary Christmas cake.

"Why did ya cut the cake Pet?"

"I… I didn't. It was piping hot before you knocked on the door. It was right there,"

"Are ya sure Pet? I thought only yesterday I had made myself a sandwich and ate it, turned out I made myself some soup and binned it instead,"

Jane wanted to say how old, silly and forgetful Marg had become in her old age, but as much as she wanted to, Jane loved her best friend far, far too much to be that mean to her.

"That didn't happen,"

"Good Pet, because you would look like a right idiot for doing that,"

Jane just smiled as she stood up and went over to the cake. It looked perfectly cooked in the middle with perfect fruit distribution and the most perfect crumb Jane had ever seen. This was going to be an amazing cake on Christmas day.

It was just annoying that someone had dared to steal some from her!

"Shut that window pet please,"

Jane nodded and looked at the window and she just folded her arms. This was getting ridiculous, the window earlier than only been opened a little bit but now it was wide open, letting a massive draft come in.

Jane went into one of her cupboards and took out some plain flour, sprinkling it around the window to check for fingerprints.

There were none.

But there was the top of a black leather glove caught in-between the window and the hinges. Jane carefully took it out and smelt it. The awful scents of cheap female perfume filled her nose as she passed it to Marg to examine.

"This ain't good Pet," Marg said, "someone stole my cake,"

Jane laughed and she agreed. Marg was always her first taste tester and… oh that was why Marg had come round today, and Jane just playfully hit Marg on the head.

"Figured it out then Pet?"

"You're terrible,"

"I'm hungry that's what pet,"

As Jane went into the cupboard and got Marg a pack of biscuits, she couldn't help but feel her stomach tighten at the idea that someone had stolen some cake from her.

And for what?

Jane had to figure it out, because she couldn't fail her family for Christmas, she had to get the Christmas cake back from the thief or she feared more than anything else, that Christmas would be ruined for her family.

And Jane hated that idea.

***

After finishing her wonderful cup of strong tea that was so strong it almost burnt her mouth, Jane sat at the round table in her kitchen and wondered about the piece of ripped glove.

It didn't seem right in the slightest, it was clear that it had come from the thief, but what Jane couldn't understand was why steal the cake in the first place? And why only take half of it?

Jane watched Marg finish off her packet of biscuits and she almost wished she hadn't had given them to Marg, she loved those chocolate biscuits and now she was out.

"You know Pet," Marg said, "the thief was clever not to take it all,"

Jane cocked her head. "How?"

"Cos I knew you were making the cake today. If I walked in Pet, and the cake wasn't here, I would have known,"

Jane was actually surprised at her friend's logic and maybe that was the key to it. Jane couldn't remember if she had told anyone else about her famous Christmas cake, or where she and Marg were when Jane told Marg about the cake baking today?

Maybe other people could have heard.

"Where were we when I told you?" Jane asked.

"I donna Pet. Maybe the corner shop two days ago," Marg said nodding.

Jane completely agreed as that was when she had picked up an extra packet of icing because she doubted the pre-roll stuff she bought would be big enough for when she iced it in a few weeks.

"The corner shop wasn't very busy, was it?"

Marg finished off her tea. "No Pet. It was you, me and... Bourbon Creams too and the shop keeper,"

Jane clicked her fingers at Marg, she had actually spoken to the woman everyone in the village called Bourbon Creams because whenever anyone saw her, the woman always carried round and offered everyone a Bourbon Cream from her tub.

"Do you think she stole my cake?" Jane asked.

"Ha!" Marg shouted by accident. "Come on Pet, she only eats Bourbon Creams, she doesn't eat cake. And she's gluten free or something,"

Jane's eyes widened as she realised why Bourbon Creams' biscuits always tasted so amazing.

"Do you think she told anyone?"

"Yes," Marg said, "Pet, remember when you caused the massive cake fight of 99 at the cooking club before Christmas?"

Jane slowly nodded, she had completely forgotten about all the cakes that had been thrown, kicked and smashed that fateful night on New Years eve 1999.

"Well Pet, some of the ladies never forgave you for winning the cake of the Century award. Two of those women are still alive and Bourbon Creams eats with them weekly,"

"Weekly?" Jane asked, "As in the past few days,"

"Oh yes Pet," Marg said as she went over to the kettle, "I saw them yesterday in the little Turkish place off the high street. They were talking about

Christmas cakes, come to think of it,"

Jane couldn't believe these awful women would want to steal from her. But Jane could understand it all, because on New Years Eve 1999, the two women (sisters actually) have both baked their own famous sponge cakes, and then Jane turned up with her leftover Christmas Cake and won.

Jane smiled as she remembered how furious they had gotten about it all, she was fairly sure her husband even got a broken nose out of it, those two sisters were vicious.

"Smell this again," Jane said, passing Marg the glove as she sat back down with a freshly made cup of tea.

Marg smelt it. "Yea pet, that what they smell like,"

Jane stood up and smiled. This was exactly the sort of thing she needed and wanted, she was going to go to those sisters and get her cake back, Jane was never going to allow these people to spoil Christmas for her family.

Jane was going to get the cake back (and answers) no matter what.

Even if she had to be unladylike about it!

***

With Marg shuffling behind her, Jane marched up to the black front door of where the Sisters lived and pounded on it hard.

Jane was furious.

The sisters lived in such an ugly part of the

village with its rundown houses and even the sisters' stone house was cracking and falling apart. Jane was going to make them pay for stealing from her! That was a promise, not a threat!

After a few moments, the door opened and two large brutish looking women stepped outside. Jane hated their saggy-muscular builds and their poorly aged face and long grey hair.

Jane had thought they looked great last century, but they clearly hadn't been looking after themselves.

The slightly taller sister frowned at Jane. "What you want!"

Jane had to force herself not to run away, the idea of these two women beating her up kept playing through her mind, but she had to stay firm and get back her cake.

"Give me my cake back. I know you stole it. I can prove it,"

"Bugger off," the sisters said.

They went to shut the door and Jane slammed her foot in-between the door and the frame.

Pain flooded up her leg but she forced her face not to show it.

"Bugger off!" the sisters shouted as they cracked their knuckles.

"Come on Pets don't be stupid," Marg said shuffling up behind Jane.

The sisters smiled. "Two on two. That's a bit fairer,"

Jane forced Marg back as the two sisters walked

out of their house, cracking their knuckles. Jane wasn't going to let them hurt Marg.

"Stop Pets!" Marg shouted.

The two sisters' eyes widened. Jane turned around to see Marg taking out a little black device with a red flashing light on it.

"What that?" the sisters asked.

"If I press this, the police come. It's an OAP distress signal, it's a powerful thing, I always take it with me Pets," Marg said.

The sisters looked at each other. "We'll knock 'em out before that happens,"

Marg gestured she was going to press it. "I'll do it Pets. Don't be such mugs,"

Jane really didn't know what to do, she knew Marg was lying, but she had to save herself, Marg and save Christmas for her family. She just didn't know how.

The Sisters walked forward.

"I pressed it!" Marg shouted as the red flashing light got faster and faster.

The Sisters looked around. They were sweating. One of them rushed into the house.

"Give us the recipe and we'll square," the remaining sister said.

Jane shook her head. "No, my grandmother gave me the recipe and you stole from me. If you had asked, I would have given it to you, but not now. Not ever,"

The remaining sister spat at Jane's feet. "Don't

need it anyway. We ate it. It good. Now bugger off,"

As the other sister rushed back out of the house, holding a tiny piece of something in tin foil, Jane felt her stomach tighten as she knew she had failed. That half of her Christmas cake was gone.

The sisters vomited.

Jane shot back.

She covered Marg's eyes.

The sisters kept vomiting.

Vomit painted the pathway.

As the sounds of sirens filled the air, Jane's eyes widened as she watched the two sisters drop to their knees in front of their own house as they gasped for air in-between the violent waves of vomiting.

Jane smiled as two police officers walked past and just looked at Jane and Marg.

"Be a dear officer and call an ambulance," Jane said.

***

As Jane took out a brand new cake from the oven and placed it on a wire cooling rack on her kitchen worktop, she couldn't believe how amazing the air smelt, hints of warming spices, rich fruit and almost no alcohol filled the air as Jane went back over to the little table in the kitchen.

Marg was sitting there nursing a large mug of coffee as if it was whiskey, but after hearing back from the police officers and watching them siege all Jane's alcohol, she knew both of them would stay far, far, far away from alcohol this Christmas season.

It turned out Jane had misread the recipe and added in extreme levels of alcohol, and all her alcohol had gone off and turned bad, so it was no surprise to the paramedics that after eating half the Christmas cake, the two sisters had vomited.

And in reality Jane was extremely glad the theft had taken place, if the sisters hadn't stolen the cake then maybe Marg, herself and even Jane's amazing family would have been sick.

Jane shook those thoughts away, she couldn't handle the idea of anything bad happening to any of them, she loved Marg as much as her own children. She was part of the family, Jane was never ever going to let anything happen to her.

But at least sisters had learnt consequences for their actions, they were clearly horrible people and Jane (as bad as it sounded) was glad they had been violently sick, no one got to mess with her Christmas, Marg or her family and got to get away with it without punishment.

Then Jane noticed Marg was smiling at her and flicking her eyes between Jane and the Christmas Cake, if it had been anyone else, Jane would have said no. But this was Marg, her amazing friend that she would do anything for and protect until the end.

As Jane went over to the cake and cut them both a small slice, she realised this was going to be a great start to an amazing holiday season.

INTRODUCTION

Genre/ Mood: Light Crime With Romantic Elements

Enough with all this goody too shoes rubbish about the holiday season, the month of December isn't all about goodness, light and the family.

Sometimes it's about darker topics, like theft, crime and stealing, because this is a wonderful time of year for the darker side of humanity to show itself.

And that is what we have in the next story in the Holiday Extravaganza as we celebrate National Letter Writing Day in a wonderful criminal style.

You'll enjoy this one!

CHRISTMAS, CRIME, LETTER

Elizabeth State was dead, but now she lives again.

Of course she wasn't really, that would just be silly. But in a strange way she was alive once more through me, as it was her identity that my guy gave me for tonight's rather… lavish party and my theft.

I stood in the massive white room with walls reaching high into the sky and stretching as far back as I could see, and in the middle of the room there was a rather… interesting (tasteless) column with two sets of stone stairs spiralling around that, leading to two exhibition rooms.

My targets.

Now I called this the opening area of the British Museum (there probably was an official name but I didn't care).

If I was alone in here then I would definitely have taken advantage, stealing from the food court that was on the far, far side of the room and maybe even stealing from the gift shop that was rumoured to be around here.

But sadly I wasn't.

I was surrounded by the snobs of the almighty rich and powerful of the Museum's largest donators, and when I mean largest I do mean it. I don't know how some of these donators would fit on their private jets or even get into buildings. They were walking, talking, smelly tanks.

Thankfully they were some thinner donators too!

Yet I must admit watching most of these stunning fit rich men in their tight black suits, smooth faces and expensive haircuts, it was almost enough to make a woman fluster and turn red.

But I am nothing short of professional. I am here to do a theft after all.

I grabbed a glass of golden champagne and circulated through the crowd, since the most amateur mistake you can make is to survey the entire room from one spot. That's what all the security guards watch for.

The sounds of the rich men and women talking, laughing and snorting filled my ears as I circulated the room. Looking out for security guards, undercovers and any more surprises.

Now my theft was marvellous because in the spirit of National Letter Writing Day (in the US at least), the Museum had decided to host some silly party for their largest (and thinnest) donators to unveil the first ever letter written to Father Christmas, or whatever the German for Father Christmas is, as it was apparently written there.

Normally I never ever bother with such small prizes. I'm more into sparkling, dazzling and millionaire treasures, but my client mentioned that the letter was worth a few million to him, so who was I to argue with such a refined (and foul) character?

And because this theft is technically for a wonderful holiday, I bought my small golden purse packed with a few wonderful surprises for anyone who tries to stop me.

Anyway I need a few quid these days for my sick mother, so I'm not exactly in a position to be too fussy with work. Then the rest of the money I'll probably keep some, donate some more to charity. I might even donate some to the museum.

Ha! Fat chance!

The sound of people shuffling caught my attention as I followed the crowds of (hot) young men and some other women towards the front of the room. Then I simply glided to the back of the crowd so I could watch everyone as we all stared at this posh elderly man who stood (way too) proudly on the stone steps.

I coughed a few times as I smelt all the horrible scents of aftershaves, perfumes and whatever unholy concoction these rich snobs covered their bodies in. I mean this is just ridiculous. A few sprays is fine fair enough, but an entire bottle! I don't want to choke to death on their smell!

As the elderly man starting to thank the donators, making a few awful jokes that only the snobbish manners of the rich would understand and introducing the letter. I started to notice a rather stunning man standing next to me.

He looked amazing in his custom-made tight black suit, his smooth handsome face and his stunning movie star smile. He seemed to be listening intently to the elderly man, but I didn't recognise him.

You see, I always make it a job before a job to memorise everyone's faces so I know exactly who will be there.

This hot guy wasn't meant to be here.

A drop of sweat rolled down my back. Now I had to play it cool, I couldn't act rash or question this guy because he would know what I was. And if he wasn't another thief then that would be a major cock-up on my part.

Believe me I may have done that before. Not a good idea.

The man leant closer to me. "You look beautiful tonight,"

If this man was simply a rich donator who wanted to unzip my dress then that would be okay, but there was something about this guy.

"Don't look so bad yourself," I said.

"What's your plan to get the letter? I was thinking about a simple fire alarm trick," the man said.

This guy might have been a thief, or he was lying which was my guess, but he couldn't have been a very good one given the letter was stored in a protected environment and extra security protocols were activated by the fire alarm.

"I don't know what you're talking about," I said, focusing on the speaker who looked like he was wrapping up.

"Who have you come as this time, Madame Francis?"

I felt my smile disappear as he said the name of one of my old aliases, he must have known of me for ages considering that one was from a job in France maybe… five years ago. At least I still had my escape routes if needed.

The stunning man stepped in front of me and

looked at my name badge, not that it would give him anything too useful.

"Elizabeth State, good name. She died ten years ago in the Caribbean you know,"

Now I ready wanted to leave, this guy knew way, way, way too much for being a simple rich man at a party. The man felt safe and good enough but there was something about him. He was hot as hell and yes, I would love him to unzip my dress tonight, but there was something off.

I went close to his ears, savouring the amazing smell of his aftershave.

"I presume you're a cop,"

The man almost laughed. "No, no Elizabeth. I not a cop. I see you haven't got my letter yet,"

I took a few steps back. This man couldn't have been my client, on the phone my client sounded older, richer and nowhere near as sexy.

The man kept smiling and changed his voice.

"In the package there will be an invitation and a dress. Go to the party, get the target and drop it off on the third seat of the Ten O'clock Tube at the nearest station,"

This wasn't right. They were the exact words of my client, but now this made no sense to me. I was well renowned as a master thief and yet my client felt the need to tail me to this event. They must have known I could get the letter-

The elderly man finished and started leading everyone up into the exhibition hall where the letter was.

I and this stunning but annoying as hell man followed.

"I wasn't expecting you here. But my fee is

doubled," I said.

The man frowned.

"I did tell you on my website. No tails. You must have read the terms and conditions?"

The man muttered something.

In truth I didn't have any terms, conditions or contracts on the site, but my clients always believed it. The amazing stupidity of the rich!

The crowd led me into a slightly smaller white room with the walls covered in breath-taking depictions of Christmas traditions through the centuries. From the pagans that started Christmas as we know it all the way to the wonderful (and far better) secular Christmases that we all know and love today, in all but name.

As the crowd of rich men and women slowly went around the room reading the stuff on the walls, my eyes were immediately drawn to the large glass cabinet in the middle of the room.

And inside it was a large, very long letter to Father Christmas in perfect condition and all written in German.

It was hard to believe that such a thing was worth so much money, but this hot as hell man clearly wanted it.

Then the idiot hot man decided to start walking straight over to the letter. Idiot!

I went over to him, wrapped my arm round his and guided him away.

"Oh honey, wait. We can look at the letter later, I want to read about Pagan festivals first," I said, shaking my head and smiling at my pretend lover.

The man smiled and went close to my ear. "What are you doing?"

"Oh honey, you've never done this before have you,"

"Never,"

If this was any other guy, I would easily make up some lame excuse to take him outside, then I would hit him, because this is my operation, my theft, my life and this idiot was going to muck it up.

Sadly this man was way too hot to hit and I wished I run my hands under that tight amazing suit and through his wonderfully thick hair, and his lips looked so soft, so warm, so-

The man started to guide me back over to the letter. This was getting out of hand.

"Listen," I said firmly. "No self-respecting thief goes for the prize straight away. That is how you get caught,"

The man stopped, kissed my head and pretended to talk about the pagan festivals.

"And I can see exactly what I need from here," I said.

"Like what?"

"There are five security guards. One in each corner and an undercover by the letter. The ones in the corners aren't a problem. The crowd is too thick and would delay them,"

"Who's the problem?" the man said, a little too enthusiastically for my taste.

"The one in the middle. He would get to us too quick,"

The man rubbed my arm as a few people looked at us. My fingers against my arm felt amazing, pure electricity flowed through me, I was enjoying him way too much.

"What about the glass cabinet itself? Looks

harmless," he asked.

Again if this was anyone else, I would have told them to break the cabinet, whilst I slipped into the crowd and let them get arrested. But sadly this stunning man was actually growing on me.

"Don't be stupid. The cabinet is electrified, it has a motion sensor and a heat sensor built into the case,"

The man frowned. "I thought you could break it,"

Now that was offensive!

"What do you take me for?" I asked.

"A hack,"

How I didn't slap him then I don't know.

A tall waitress was coming towards us with glasses of wonderfully golden champagne.

"Grab a glass," I said firmly.

We both grabbed one.

I couldn't help my smile but the next part was going to be great fun. Normally I did the whole acting chaos stuff with actual strangers but it might be even more fun acting with a person who I actually found attractive.

This was going to be fun.

"Are you a good actor?" I asked.

The man looked more concerned. "I suppose so. I did a few school plays. Lead role,"

Oh yes, this man was definitely rich. Only the rich snobs of the world ever compare school plays with proper acting and the level of acting needed for cons.

"Just play along. Go over and stand by the letter," I said.

We went over. Now the fun could begin!

I went over to him. "What are you doing! You

are so obsessed with this stupid letter!"

"Go away woman. Leave me alone for once in your miserable life. In fact. Get a life!"

"How dare you! I didn't even want to come to this shit hole museum tonight!" I shouted.

"Just go. Go back to our sorry ass kids. They're yours anyway. I don't want you, I don't want them. Now leave!"

The crowd muttered stuff.

"Maybe I will. Maybe I'll get a divorce!"

I went closer to the glass cabinet.

"Do whatever and take those bitching kids with you!"

The crowd didn't like that.

The security guards came over.

The man threw the champagne glass at me.

I ducked.

It splashed over the glass cabinet.

The security guards grabbed him. Taking him outside.

He smiled.

I pretended to cry and the elderly man in his tight suit from his speech on the steps came over and rubbed my back.

"Miss, I am so sorry you had to go through that,"

I hugged him. "And I'm so sorry for those horrible words I said. Your museum is lovely,"

I wiped a few tears away.

"Thank you. Now please stay and enjoy yourself. All five security guards will be downstairs making sure he stays away,"

As the elderly man left, I actually felt a little sad that that hot as hell stunning man wasn't going to be allowed back in. I was actually missing him!

But I did have a job to do, so onto stage two.

I went over to the glass cabinet and double checked if it was possible to see if any of the champagne had got inside.

It wasn't possible to tell. Good!

A rich young couple stood next to me so I whispered to them.

"I think the letter's damaged. I think there's champagne in there,"

The young woman looked horrified. She was clearly a history and art buff so she was perfect for this part. She rushed off to find the elderly man.

When she returned she was in a terrible (to her, wonderful to me) state and was begging the elderly man to open the glass cabinet to check on the *historical integrity* of the letter (Oh yes, she was one of those people).

The elderly man took out a key card from his suit pocket and swiped it over the glass cabinet. The cabinet hummed, vibrated and hissed as the pressurised air escaped. Making the air smell horribly of mustard.

Then the elderly man took off the glass and exposed the letter for all to see.

This was my chance.

I opened my gold purse, cracked a vial and waited.

The elderly man inspected the letter without picking it up.

The young woman and man were talking to the elderly man. He was distracted, my exit was clear.

I grabbed a small breath refresher from my purse filled with knock gas and I sprayed the three of them.

I grabbed the letter.

And run out.

I run down the stairs, past the security guards and out into the night.

***

A few hours later I stood on the cold lonely platform of the Tube Station with no one else there and only the cold concrete and white tiled walls to keep me company. Like every Tube Station after hours, the station smelt like urine, sick and spoiled food, but there was something refreshing about it tonight.

The foul smell kept me alert as I waited for the train and then I could easily escape into the chaos of London, change my identity and begin anew.

If it sounded like a lonely life, that was because it was in a way. It was partly why I did these jobs, thefts and other crazy things, because it meant I got to meet people and experience things that I never would be able to otherwise.

But tonight was surprisingly nice actually. I had never wanted to spend time with anyone before but that hot sexy man with his tight black suit, smooth handsome face and his amazing haircut. I really, really wanted him.

I wanted him to unzip my dress, run my fingers through his hair and down his suit to where my parcel could be delivered.

But I guess that was never going to happen, so again I would be alone doing random jobs over Christmas trying to raise more money for my sick mother, myself and the various charities that I'll donate to.

The sound of the Tube train in the distance made me step towards the edge of the platform as I waited for it to arrive when an arm wrapped round my waist.

I would recognise that amazing aftershave and those strong arms anywhere. That hot, sexy man had returned to me.

"You did well. My Letter?" the man asked.

I smiled and passed him the letter.

He ripped it up.

"What!" I shouted, as the pieces of the letter blew across the rails.

"Relax beautiful. The Letter's fake. I wrote it, aged it and donated it to the Museum. I only wanted to check if it was a good enough forgery,"

All I could do was stare at that amazing movie star smile as he probably felt really pleased with himself, and I couldn't blame him. Fooling the British Museum was no easy feat but he had to be here for something.

"You think I'm beautiful?" I asked.

As the train rolled into the station, the driver probably shocked that there were people here at all, that amazing hot sexy man kissed me on the lips. Hard. I savoured his soft lips and wondered what else was he hiding.

But at least I had my answer. He did find me beautiful, and I him.

I was half expecting him to say something but he gave me a smile. Not a malice, deceptive or evil smile that I would have expected for a forger and fellow criminal. But a smile that a schoolboy gives his prom date when he truly loves her.

He might have been a strange, hot, sexy criminal man who I barely knew, but as the train doors opened and we both went on, I looked forward to seeing where the train was going to lead us and hopefully our journey wouldn't end for a long, long time.

INTRODUCTION
Mood/ Genre: Fun Private Eye Mystery

As we move on to our second Bettie English mystery of the Extravaganza, I wanted to take an extremely personal aspect of the holiday season and morph it into a great mystery story.

Since we all have some sort of social party, event or other thing going on in the holiday season. You might have a work's do, an office Christmas party or something special you do with your friends every year.

Personally, I always tend to go out with friends before Christmas as a little pre-Christmas celebration, in addition to the university Christmas socials that happen in early December, and those are great fun!

But my point is there are little social events that are unique to each group that make the holiday season extra special to each of us.

So how do Private Eyes celebrate such things?

Well that is the great focus of this short mystery

story, so please expect an enthralling fun story about everyone's favourite Private Eye as she prepares for one of the most important events in the Private Eye calendar.

And if you want to see Bettie and her team at the most important Private Eye event of the year, please check out the gripping, unputdownable book *The Federation Protects* available at all major booksellers from August 2023.

Enjoy!

PRIVATE EYE, CONVENTION AND CHRISTMAS

"What's EyeFoodCon aunty?"

When Bettie heard her nephew Sean ask her that simple question, she wasn't really sure how to answer it. As a private eye she had just known what it was for as long as she could remember.

Bettie looked at her tall slim nephew and tried to think about how to answer such a strange question, that she knew what it was, she just didn't know how to explain it to someone who wasn't a private eye.

The sounds of people talking, chatting and laughing on the awfully cold December night made Bettie shiver. She hated the cold so she pulled her long black overcoat tighter and ignored her nephew.

As much as Bettie loved him, she wanted, needed to buy herself a few extra seconds so she could think of an answer to his question.

Bettie watched the little families walk around with the occasional parent moaning at their overexcited kids and other people were weighed down with their Christmas shopping in Bluewater shopping centre in southeast England.

She was glad her and Sean hadn't bought that much stuff tonight but she did need to press on with their shopping. That was probably the only downside to the Christmas season, even more so as a private eye, there were so many cases at Christmas time that it made Christmas shopping in advance impossible.

Bettie bit her lip as she wondered how many more presents she needed to buy. There was her sister, her boyfriend and more.

As she pushed those panicked thoughts away, Bettie watched the busy crowd around them go in and out of shops like their lives depended on it, it seemed them too needed to get lots of presents before the big day.

The smell of rich Christmas spices filled the air as Bettie and Sean kept walking on, gliding through the crowd and walking like they were on a mission. Because in a way they were, Bettie had to get all the presents tonight considering the all the private eye parties started soon.

With the smell of the Christmas spices getting stronger with hints of sweat that made her mouth taste of Christmas cake, Bettie kept gliding through the crowd as her eyes narrowed for the next shop she needed.

"What's EyeFoodCon aunty?" Sean asked again walking next to her.

Bettie smiled. "It's hard to explain Sean. It's a little private holiday for private eyes,"

"Is it like a Christmas party?"

Bettie stepped out of the way of a big family of shoppers and saw a massive wonderful sign in the distance of a perfume shop she needed to go to for her sister. She had no idea why her sister wanted some expensive perfume that she was never going to wear, but Bettie just wanted to keep the peace, love her sister and get on with the rest of the shopping.

The only problem was the sea of busy (grumpy) shoppers in her way.

"Aunty?" Sean asked.

Bettie took Sean's hand like she did when he was a toddler and guided him through the sea of people.

"In a way yes," Bettie said. "It was started a few years back by the Jewish and Muslim private eyes,"

Bettie gently knocked a shopper out of the way so her and Sean could continue through the crowd.

"They heard all their private eye friends were busy and missing over Christmas as they were celebrating with the family. So the Professional Private Investigator Society created EyeFoodCon as a secular celebration for everyone,"

"Ah," Sean said.

After making it through the massive sea of grumpy, busy shoppers, Bettie loved the amazing smell of the sweet flowery perfume in the massive shop she entered.

Bettie cocked her head for a moment as she

didn't remember the shop being this big before, but she loved the long white walls of colour perfume bottles in all their different shapes, sizes and prices.

She wanted to shake her head when she saw Sean walk over to the unisex (but more feminine) perfume as she knew for a fact that he was getting it for himself.

The smell of the sweet flowery perfume kept getting stronger but Bettie knew something was off. It was too strong for someone just spraying.

Bettie stared at the horribly shiny white floor and her eyes widened when she saw a smashed bottle of perfume a few metres from her.

She walked over and had to cover her nose with her hand, Bettie normally loved that perfume but it was way too strong when she was breathing in a whole bottle of it.

"You're going to have to pay for that Miss," a woman said.

Bettie looked at the tall business-like woman who had said that, and she shook her head. It was silly that this woman thought Bettie had done it, she had only just got here.

"I found it like this," Bettie said.

The woman shook her head. "They all say that. Come with me and you can pay for it at the tills,"

"I didn't break it. I'm innocent. Check your cameras,"

The woman frowned. "I know what I saw,"

Bettie couldn't believe how silly this woman was,

she supposed the woman could be fed up with all the stealing and breaking that normally happens at Christmas, but Bettie wasn't guilty.

"Aunty?" Sean said walking over.

"Sean how are you?" the woman asked. "How's Harry? We have a new stock that aftershave he likes,"

Bettie wanted to shake her head so badly, trust Sean to walk into a scene and instantly know how to calm it down. That was probably why she had bought him just in case.

"Thank you, I'll take a bottle. What were you talking to my aunty about?"

Bettie couldn't believe it when the woman looked at her and explained everything to Sean like Bettie was the worse criminal ever.

Sean nodded. "I know my Aunty seems shifty, criminal and a bit crazy but she's safe,"

How Bettie didn't playfully hit him she didn't know.

"I can assure you my Aunty didn't break anything. She's honest and she could help you,"

Bettie felt like she was going to regret this for sure, maybe she should have bought her boyfriend Graham like he had suggested.

Bettie stepped forward. "Help you how,"

"Your nephew mentions you're a Private Investigator,"

As much as Bettie wanted to correct her as she loved the more playful term Private Eye, Bettie knew this probably wasn't the time considering whoever this woman was still thought she was guilty.

"Bettie English Private Eye at your service,"

The woman nodded. "Our cameras aren't working at the moment and… my boss isn't happy with me. If I hire you to watch the store for a couple of hours-"

Bettie's mouth dropped. "Wait! I have Christmas shopping to do. I have a mini-convention to buy food for and… it's Christmas soon,"

"Aunty I can do the shopping for you,"

Bettie wanted to protest but she supposed she loved Sean too much and he was being nice, but Bettie didn't want to do this.

"How much?" Bettie asked.

"We paid the last security person a hundred pounds for the night,"

Bettie didn't know whether to be shocked, pleased or horrified that a security person is actually given that much money for a few hours of work. But the sound of a hundred pounds for two little hours, it did sound good.

It was technically her turn to host and pay for most of EyeFoodCon so that money would easily pay for it.

"Hundred pounds for the night. Extra twenty for false accusations," Bettie said.

The woman frowned.

"And throw it two bottles of whatever Sean wants since you hesitated," Bettie said smiling.

"Fine. I trust you know how to look innocent

and like a random shopper,"

As she watched the woman and Sean walk off so he could choose what he wanted, Bettie looked around the massive store and rolled her eyes. Some days it really sucked to be a private eye but a hundred pounds was a hundred pounds that she didn't have before, and maybe she could find a nice present for Graham to buy her.

The advantages of borrowing his credit card earlier!

Walking up the rows of perfume bottles, Bettie didn't know how these two hours were going to go, surely a perfume shop didn't see that much crime at Christmas.

***

After an hour and forty-five minutes, Bettie couldn't believe how brilliant this actually was, at first she thought she was going to hate it with a passion, but she didn't.

Bettie had already found some great new perfumes that she loved, she found the foul smelling one that her dad loved and she even found a new special one for herself that she might wear on Christmas day.

But Bettie still didn't want to buy any of them because as much as they were great perfumes, they weren't cheap and a hundred pounds was not going to cover it. Not by a long shot.

Bettie ran her fingers over the cold white shelves as she looked at all the perfume and aftershave bottles in all their different sizes, shapes and colours. The bottles were beautiful but Bettie remembered from her business study classes at school that was all part of the visual appeal. It did nothing practical, except from increase the prices.

The sound of customers talking, trying on perfume and judging the smells echoed all around the massive shop as Bettie waited for her two hours to be up.

Yet Bettie could have sworn there was another sound she was hearing, it was like the low quiet voices of two people conspiring to do something.

Bettie had hated the idea of people stealing from the start, it was Christmas for crying out loud, this was not a time for stealing, it was a time for love, giving and caring.

Walking to the end of the shelf she was looking at, Bettie's eyes narrowed on the two young women that were close together and trying on different perfumes.

To other people they may not have looked like criminals or would-be shoplifters, but Bettie recognised the closeness, quiet voices and the long expensive coats of the two girls.

It reminded Bettie of her own troublesome streak when she was a teenager, if that was the case with these two women then Bettie supposed she could get rid of them without any major problems.

But these women weren't teenagers, they were fully-fledged adults who were looking like they were going to try and steal something.

After a few moments of watching, Bettie noticed that one of the women had got out her phone and was pretending to take a phone call. Bettie shook her head as she watched the perfectly clear black screen of the girl's phone, if you're going to pretend to take a pretend phone call you need to make it a bit more convincing.

Bettie wondered if she should get the woman or the manager to deal with them, but she wasn't going to risk losing her hundred pounds for simply *failing* to do her assigned job. She wasn't risking any comments like that.

As the woman with the phone pretended to nod, promise the person on the other side of the call she'd take a picture and check the surroundings (completely missing Bettie). Bettie knew that this woman was an amateur, there was no way these two had done shoplifting before.

If Bettie was doing this she would have been in the car park driving home by now.

Then Bettie watched in horror as the two women did a final check of the store, missed Bettie and just picked up the perfumes like it was nothing and placed it in their coat pockets.

Bettie walked towards them. The two women pretended to act normal.

"I know what you just did," Bettie said.

"We ain't steal nothing," the pretend phone caller said.

Bettie shook her head. "I finish my 'shift' in two minutes. I do not want to be here any longer than I have to be. Just apologise, pay for the perfumes and go,"

"We ain't steal nothing," they both said together.

Bettie hated this entire thing, she had Christmas shopping to do, EyeFoodCon to plan and buy for and on top of all of that she no longer wanted to be in some perfume shop.

"Empty your pockets," Bettie said firmly.

The two women ran.

Bettie ran after them.

Her feet pounded the floor.

The two women were fast.

Bettie couldn't let them leave the shop.

She looked around.

The women were close to the exit.

There were a sea of shoppers.

Bettie was going to lose them.

Bettie panicked.

Picked up a perfume bottle.

Threw it.

It smashed on the woman's back.

She fell forward.

Catching the other woman.

There was something oddly satisfying around that Bettie realised as she walked over and stood over the two injured women were who frowning and probably wished they had tried another shop.

The tall business-like woman ran over to Bettie.

"Miss English! What have you done?"

"These two women were stealing. I stopped them. You own me my hundred pounds,"

"You damaged my store! You broke a bottle of perfume! You…"

Bettie shook her head. "My hundred pounds and extra twenty please. Or I will call your head office and tell them you hired a private eye on company time and money without approval,"

Bettie couldn't help but smile as the woman looked so shocked and panicked as if this was the first time ever she had been challenged.

"Fine Miss English," the woman said giving Bettie her money.

"Let's do this again some time," Bettie said leaving the shop.

"Let's not," Bettie heard the woman muttered.

The moment she left the shop, Bettie glided into the sea of busy grumpy shoppers and called Sean. As the phone dialled she was slightly surprised how good she was feeling after all of that, it felt great to be out in December, doing her shopping and stopping crime at the same time.

But now she had to get on with the most important event in the Private Eye calendar, EyeFoodCon.

Sean picked up his phone.

Bettie smiled. "Hi Sean, want to come to EyeFoodCon with me?"

***

A few days later Bettie sat on a terribly cold chair on the head of a long, long oak table with wonderfully decorated Christmas decorations covering the entire walls.

Bettie loved all their baubles, tinsel and the wreaths that covered the walls of the business room that she had hired especially for the convention.

And as she watched all the different Private Eyes in all their different ethnicities, sizes and heights eat the beautiful golden, crispy food in front of them, and the rest of the juicy meats and other sweet treats that covered the entire length of the table, Bettie realised something precious.

The sound of happy Private Eyes talking, chatting and laughing with one another reminded Bettie how EyeFoodCon should be explained to anyone.

Bettie looked at Sean who was laughing with a young woman at the table and he saw her.

Bettie leaned closer to Sean. "You see all this,"

Sean looked around and nodded.

"This is what EyeFoodCon is all about. No matter your race, religion, preferences, whatever. You are always welcome in the Private Eye community. We are all a family,"

Sean smiled at that.

"So what is EyeFoodCon you ask," Bettie said.

Sean leant closer.

"EyeFoodCon is about community and the secular side of Christmas. I love all Private Eyes no matter who they are and I welcome them all. This mini-convention is a reminder of that at this time of year,"

Sean looked around a final time.

"Just because we don't all celebrate Christmas doesn't mean we can't love, give and support each other at this time of year,"

Just saying that made Bettie feel all Christmassy and merry because she knew that was all the truth, and that's why she loved being a Private Eye because it truly was a community.

A loving, supporting and amazing community for all.

Bettie was a bit surprised when Sean kissed her cheek and held her hands.

"Merry Christmas Aunty,"

Bettie stood up and said to everyone: "A Merry Christmas, New Year and all the other celebrations to everyone,"

INTRODUCTION
Mood/ Genre: Light Private Eye Mystery

I welcome you to our second Bettie English short story with the promise of amazing food, a great plot and a very good ending.

During the holiday season, everyone wants to go out for dinner, see their loved ones and enjoy spending time together.

If you and your partner spend Christmas apart out of choice or family commitments, you might go out for dinner before Christmas so you get to treat each other.

Personally the food is a favourite part of the Holidays for me, so eating out is a good pastime for this time of year as I see friends and family that I won't see on the big day itself.

Well!

If you're a Private Eye, then you never just go out for dinner, so definitely expect even more amazing food, a crime and everyone's favourite

Private Eye: Bettie English!
You'll really enjoy this mystery short story!

CHEATER AT DINNER

Surrounded by rows upon rows of stunning white tables with their perfectly pressed napkins, posh cutlery and people sitting there dressed in stunning suits and dresses, Bettie English, private eye, turned her head and focused on her table.

As she breathed in the amazing smells of rich meats, expensive fruity wine and freshly steamed vegetables, Bettie couldn't help but smile as she stared at the most amazing plate of food she had ever seen.

She loved how the traditional British Christmas dinner looked like an expensive painting on the plate with its golden crispy roast potatoes, stunningly sliced juicy pork and Bettie's favourite the succulent, vibrant colours of the vegetables on the side.

Bettie could almost taste how crispy and vibrant the vegetables' flavours would be from here, their amazing sweetness would be sheer perfection against the juiciness and meaty flavours of the pork.

The sound of people talking, chatting and laughing all around Bettie made her force her attention away from the amazing, stunning food and on the equally beautiful person she was with.

As she looked up from the plate (longing to taste the delicious dinner), she saw her cop boyfriend Graham smiling at her as he poured a fruity red wine into her glass.

A part of her wondered if she should get him to stop, but she was here as a private eye and a girlfriend, so she might well blend in.

Watching her beautiful boyfriend with his perfect hair, jawline and body, Bettie took a few shallow breaths of the amazingly scented air as she knew this was going to be a perfect evening. She had a delicious dinner (that she really wanted to eat) and the love of her life, which she hadn't seen for a few weeks.

When Graham put the wine bottle down, they both just stared at each other for a few seconds and Bettie loved that. She knew it probably looked weird to other people but she loved all the time she spent with (and admiring) Graham.

The sound of cheering filled the restaurant so Bettie turned, smiled and her eyes narrowed as she looked at a couple who were hugging and kissing and everyone was clapping around them.

She knew they had just gotten engagement and a part of Bettie admired the man was being so ballsy and proposing in public. Bettie was still getting used to the whole relationship thing with Graham, but she loved him and he her.

Marriage might have been a long time away, but Bettie wanted it one day, one day far from now.

Then Bettie saw Graham cross his arms and smiled.

"So why ya wanna come here?" Graham asked.

Bettie gave him a massive smile. "What do you mean? Can't a girl take her man out on the town?"

"A girl or woman can. You don't,"

Bettie pretended to be offended and they both laughed.

That sole reason was why Bettie loved him and she would give anything to always see that amazing smile of his.

But he did have a point she supposed, they were always working, busying and helping others so much that they often forgot to work on each other, in more ways than one.

And tonight was no different.

"Look my left and tell me what you see," Bettie said.

She watched Graham carefully as he subtly turned his head and his eyes narrowed on a table.

"What the two dudes in the business suits?" Graham asked.

Bettie looked left and shook her head. "No,"

As she subtly pointed with her eyes at another table, and when Graham smiled she knew he had seen what they were looking for.

Mr Nero Alessandria was apparently some hotshot new businessman in London but Bettie had seen some of his speeches and companies, she wasn't that impressed but given that his wife had paid her a few thousand pounds to follow him, Bettie didn't really care.

It was even better that the wife had done almost all of Bettie's hard work by giving her all his contacts with pictures, addresses and phone numbers.

Bettie bit her lip a little when she remembered some of the rumours she had found online about him, apparently he was a ruthless man capable of horrible things but she hadn't seen any proof of that.

It still worried her though.

And when Bettie had found possible evidence of an affair with Mr Alessandria and the mystery woman meeting at a fancy London restaurant tonight, Bettie knew she wasn't going to refuse. Especially when her terms of employment always being the client pays for all needed costs. A fancy meal or two for getting evidence sounded like a needed cost.

Granted Bettie knew she would have to have a more compelling reason when she sent the invoice to the client.

The amazing smell of those beautifully golden, crispy roast potatoes made Bettie return her attention to the utterly stunning dinner in front of her. Bettie wasn't sure how much longer she could contain herself with that perfectly sliced juicy pork just staring at her.

"I presume ya hear for photos?" Graham asked.

Bettie nodded and subtly turn her head to focus more on the person sitting opposite him.

From where she was Bettie couldn't see too much about the woman, but it was definitely a woman. Bettie noted the woman's long blond hair, slim body and large assets. But she couldn't remember seeing anyone who matched the description in the information the wife had sent over.

"What ya waiting for then? Take some pictures?" Graham asked.

Bettie smiled, shook her head and rubbed his warm hands.

"I can't just take photos. Right now it is just a man and a woman sitting together. A lawyer would simply say it's a friend, a missing daughter or even his good looking mother,"

Graham's eyebrows rose at the last two.

"I'm not kidding," Bettie said.

Releasing Graham's hands wonderfully warm hands, Bettie picked up her posh knife and fork and sliced into the pork.

Just the ease of which the pork was cut got Bettie excited, her pork was normally rough and tough, but this… this was something else.

When she popped the pork into her mouth, she thought she was going to faint at how amazing it was. The succulent juices with their rich meaty flavours flooded her senses and the meat dissolved in her mouth.

This was going to be a night to remember.

As Bettie continued to eat the best dinner she had ever had with those golden crispy potatoes being her true favourites, she constantly flicked her eyes over to Mr Alessandria and the mystery woman.

The more Bettie focused on them, the more she couldn't understand what was going on. Even her and Graham who were working but still a loving couple, they were laughing, smiling and talking whenever they weren't eating.

But Mr Alessandria and the mystery woman weren't.

Bettie couldn't understand how they were looking at each other and barely speaking. It was almost like they weren't on a date but something else was going on.

After a while of subtly looking at them, Bettie put down her cutlery, finished off her amazing golden crispy potato and looked at Graham.

"You aren't a cop tonight are you?" Bettie asked.

Graham's eyebrows rose. "No. Why would ya ask

that?"

Bettie smiled, took out her phone and dialled a number.

"Cos I'm doing something questionable,"

"Who ya calling?"

Bettie smiled at the thought of hearing her wonderful nephew Sean who should still have been at her office with his boyfriend. She had said to him just to do her filing but Bettie knew he would have done other stuff too, which was why she hadn't cleaned her office in the past week.

"Calling Sean,"

"He and Harry wouldn't be in the office?"

Bettie smiled and just looked at him. "Two young boys alone in an office together. Away from my sister and her husband. They aren't going to be there. Seriously?"

Graham nodded and went back to eating.

Sean answered sounding a bit out of breath. "Hi Aunty,"

"Sean I'm going to send you a picture and I need you to try and find out who it is. Check the information the wife gave us first. I might have missed something,"

"Okay,"

"Thank you," Bettie said as she hung up, took a picture and send it to him.

When she turned back to Graham he had his normally ruggedly handsome cop face on.

"How you goanna identify it?"

Bettie rubbed his hand gently. "It's perfectly legal. I always save the questionable software from the dark web as a last resort,"

Graham gave her a sort of nervous chuckle and

he went back to eating his dinner. Bettie felt her body relax and tense and relax again as she realise she had just basically lied to him. As much as Bettie loved that dark web software from time to time, she knew it was 100% illegal.

But worth every penny.

Pushing those illegal thoughts away, Bettie picked up her cold glass of wine, breathed in the fruity hints and pretended to slip it.

When her eyes flicked back over to Mr Alessandria, Bettie put the wine glass down and her eyes narrowed. He was waving his finger at the woman like an angry parent would at a child.

He was clearly mad and probably struggling to keep his voice down.

Bettie wondered what he was talking about, he was a business owner so maybe it was something to do with that, but then Bettie remembered all the financial records and everything looked okay. Mr Alessandria had plenty of new investors too so he was set financially.

She had to get more information.

"Graham," Bettie said her eyes moving back to him. "Want to do a bit of acting?"

Graham frowned and Bettie smiled.

"I was wondering why I was here," Graham asked.

"Oh darling you're here because I love you. And Sean's too young to play certain roles and her sister would kill me for getting him involved too much in the Private Eye world,"

Graham shook his head. "Fine, what do you want me to do?"

"Easy. We get into a fight. I storm off towards

the target. We both take a glass of wine. We spill over them,"

"Then they go to the loos and follow 'em,"

"Exactly,"

Graham filled up the wine glasses again and giggled like a little schoolboy.

"Please Graham. Act serious," Bettie said laughing herself.

Both of them took a deep breath, made sure no one was watching and blow each other a kiss.

"You what! You sold my car!" Graham shouted.

Bettie was a bit taken back. "Well. You're useless. Lazy! I work all day and you do nothing!"

People were starting to look.

"You didn't have to sell my-"

"It isn't your car Graham. I paid for it,"

"It's our money. We're married,"

"Maybe we shouldn't be. Your mother is a such a nob too!" Bettie said.

Everyone was watching now.

Bettie shot up and grabbed the wine glass.

"Don't ya dare talk about my mother!"

"She's horrible. She hates me!" Bettie said.

She started to storm off.

"She's right Bet. I hate you too. You are so controlling!"

Bettie glided through the rows of tables.

She was almost at the target table.

Mr Alessandria stared at her and Graham.

"I wouldn't have to be so controlling. If you were useful. You gold digger!"

Graham grabbed her.

Bettie turned around.

"That's right Graham. You're a gold digger. A

dickhead. I'm leaving you!" Bettie shouted.

Throwing her wine glass.

The wine covered Mr Alessandria.

"Fine then nob!" Graham said throwing his wine over the other woman.

"You idiots!" Mr Alessandria shouted.

Bettie and Graham turned around and their hands covered their faces.

"Oh my god. I am so sorry sir," Bettie said, grabbing a napkin off a table and helping him clean it up.

Graham did the same for the woman.

"Go away. I need to clean up," Mr Alessandria said as he stood up, marched off and went into the toilets.

Bettie nodded at Graham and he left.

As she watched him go into the toilets, Bettie stared at the tall slim woman at the table and saw her just stare into space, she didn't even bother trying to clean herself up.

It was about this time Bettie realised that she hadn't needed to get wine over the mystery woman, but there was something off about her.

Sitting down on the horribly warm chair, Bettie looked at the woman and waited for her to ask why Bettie was sitting there, or how was she after the fight.

But the woman just stared.

Feeling her phone vibrate in her pocket, Bettie took it out and smiled when she saw it was a message from Sean telling her the woman was actually a new investor called Lady Penelope Bishop, some rich daughter of the English nobility.

"You don't look like a Penelope," Bettie said.

Penelope looked up at her.

"What were you two arguing about?" Bettie asked.

Bettie wondered if the woman was going to leave when her eyes kept switching between the door and Bettie, but after a few seconds Penelope stared into Bettie's eyes.

A part of Bettie felt as if Penelope was borrowing down into her soul, yet Bettie was surprised that this clearly fierce capable woman would allow Mr Alessandria to moan at her.

"Are you police?" she asked.

Bettie shook her head. "No but that is all you need to know,"

Penelope stood up. "Then whoever you are, I do not need to speak to the likes of you,"

"One scream from me and a police officer runs out of that bathroom," Bettie said coldly.

Penelope stared at her.

"I will scream. You know the lengths I go for my acting," Bettie gestured to the red wine stains on Penelope's dress.

"Fine. I am investing millions of your pounds into his company for a favour,"

Bettie's eyes narrowed, she wasn't from here and the way she said *your pounds* wasn't right, it sounded evil, dark and mysterious all at the same time.

Then the more Bettie looked at the woman, the more she realised that the woman definitely wasn't British and probably had ties to overseas crime.

"Who are you?" Bettie asked.

"I am just a businesswoman the same as you. But unlike you I presume you own your pockets. I do not. I have all the money in other pockets that I can play with,"

Bettie partly wanted to explain how her client was paying for all of this tonight, but this didn't seem like the real moment for accuracy.

"What is this favour?"

Penelope smiled and stood up. "Miss whoever you are, I urge you to go back to your table and finish. Tell your client…"

Bettie stepped forward. "How many Private Eyes have come for you?"

Penelope placed a gentle hand on Bettie's shoulder.

"So, so many. But you should know that your London is filled with opportunities and criminal gangs. So many wonderful opportunities for me and my kin to spread, work and love,"

Bettie felt a shot of icy coldness wash down her spine as she watched Penelope gather up her things and prepare to leave.

"What do I tell my client?"

"That man rejected us tonight. Don't do everything. She'll be rich soon enough,"

Bettie smiled and felt her stomach churn and tighten.

"Don't come for her," Bettie said bitterly.

Penelope stopped and stared Bettie dead in the eye. Again Bettie felt as she was having her soul burrowed into.

"You have yourself a deal. But I will call on you one day. I will find out who you are and you will do a single case for me,"

Bettie stopped and wondered if this was the only way to keep everyone safe, it didn't sound unreasonable. Her client would soon be rich but…

Bettie hated the feeling of sitting back whilst something terrible happened.

Bettie knew this woman spoke perfect English, but there was more to it, a much darker side that a part of Bettie didn't want to get involved in. She wanted to tell Graham about it, but this was out of his jurisdiction and she remembered what these gangs were like.

She had to protect Graham.

"Fine. One case. Don't come to my client for help," Bettie said then realised something. "How did you know my client was the wife?"

Penelope started to walk away but she said a final message to Bettie in perfect Russian. "We always watch,"

As Bettie stared at Penelope (or whoever she really was) walk out of the restaurant, she felt her entire stomach tighten into a knot and even the amazing smells of the perfectly sliced, juicy pork couldn't relax her.

The sound of Graham and Mr Alessandria walking up behind her made Bettie tense even more as she knew she couldn't warn Mr Alessandria in front of Graham. As much as Bettie loved him, she knew he was far too good of a cop and the last thing she wanted was him investigating the Russians.

And something deep, deep inside her knew everything would be okay in the end. The client would be rich, the questionable businessman dead and Bettie only had to do one case for a potentially dangerous Russian woman.

Bettie smiled at the craziness of it all so she shook Mr Alessandria's hand, bid him good night and walked back over to her table.

As she sat down, Bettie stared at what was left of the golden crispy potatoes, perfectly sliced juicy pork and the most amazing vibrant vegetables she had ever seen.

Picking up her cutlery, Bettie knew the food would be cold but it would still be amazing and worth every single bite.

At the sound of Graham pouring them another glass of the rich fruity wine, Bettie stared wide eyed at him as she admired his beautiful hair, face and body.

"Merry Christmas Bet,"

Bettie gave him a schoolgirl smile. "Merry Christmas Graham,"

INTRODUCTION
Mood/ Genre: Light Historical Fiction

When readers ask me where I get my ideas from? It is always such a difficult question because there are so many different sources. Sometimes I get them from real life, conversations, books and more.

However, there are other times when I get them from history and that is where the idea behind this story came from.

Personally I have always loved world war two history, because there was so much going on, there are a lot of resources on it and it is the main world war that we're taught about at school. So I have always had an interest in it.

Therefore, I was reading up on my world war two history when I came across the very strange and funny episode of a Gestapo (German Police) raid on a French resistance ally involving a maid and the house owner as mentioned in *Madame Fourcade's Secret War* by Lynne Olson. I decided I just had to do a story inspired by that precious (and rather funny) piece of history.

If you love wonderful historical fiction stories about protection, freedom and what it takes to keep it. You will definitely love today's story.

Read it now!

SALVATION IN THE MAID
13th December 1942
Northern France, Europe

Janet Berin might have just been a so-called simple country woman who served as a maid to a wealthy estate owner in Northern France but she wasn't always like that. As a child she had dreamed of grand adventures in Paris, Marseille and she had loved her schooling. Her parents had tried to give her everything they could possible, and they gave a hell of a lot.

But when the capitulation of France happened in 1940, Janet had to make a choice. She could either stay in the newly occupied regions or go into the Free zone. She was a teacher at a local girl's school and continued for a little whilst the Reich continued to consolidate its power, but when they wanted to convert the school into a base of spying operations.

Janet left.

As Janet stood by a horribly cramp little kitchen

sink made of awfully cold metal and finished washing up some potatoes for tonight's dinner. She really wondered where her life had gone, she knew she was damn well lucky to have a job at all with her being relatively free to enjoy her evening by herself.

But she missed the children, the teaching and the learning that came from being a teacher. She had of course tried to go back into teaching but it… it wasn't what it was like before.

The Nazis wanted her to teach innocent children about how grand Germany and Hilter was and how everything else was awful.

Janet couldn't do it, and now she was a maid for a good man called Reuben Portia, a wealthy businessman.

Janet didn't like the sheer coldness of the freezing water as she continued washing the potatoes that she had ever so carefully grown in the back garden over the summer and stored over the winter. She just hoped she would have enough for Christmas Day in a few weeks.

The smell of a watery tomato sauce with some scraps of leftovers from the Master's dinner was boiling away for her own dinner tonight. As much as Janet knew the Reuben would allow her to have a "real" dinner, she just didn't feel comfortable.

She had carefully heard what the Master and his strange friends had been talking about recently. The fall of Vichy, the crackdown on the French resistance networks and the increasing danger of France were all worrying.

If anything happened Janet just wanted to make sure Reuben had enough food to survive. He had given her so much when no one else wanted a simple country woman who used to teach little children.

The tiny window of cold natural light shone through behind her and Janet wished it was the summer once again so her ageing back would be warmed through before she had to finish her cleaning duties for the day.

Janet was about to get out her excuse of a chopping broad when people pounding the wooden front door echoed around the house.

Because the potatoes needed to dry and because she wanted to look very busy for Reuben, she threw the dripping wet potatoes into her apron and held the bottom of the apron to create a makeshift bag to carry them in.

Then to prevent Master from getting mad Janet swore under her breath as she walked up the little stairs to the ground floor (her little kitchen was almost buried underground in a former cellar). Then she went through the massive estate house with her ageing feet tapping on the hardwood floor as she went.

After passing plenty of very maintained and perfectly cleaned rooms filled with expensive furniture, photos and decorations that she polished each day. She made it to the very large wooden door where the pounding was coming from.

"Police!" someone shouted.

Janet carefully wiped her hands on her little apron, took a deep breath of the cold crispy air and opened the door.

She was flat out amazed all the potatoes were still in her little makeshift apron bag.

Janet had to control herself when she saw the three Gestapo German officers standing there. Their expression were as hard as a person's could get, they looked furious and like they were hunting something or something.

They easily towered over Janet.

"Yes?" Janet asked.

"We have been authorised to search this estate in search of resistance activity," the shortest of the Germans said forcing their way into the house.

Janet had no idea what he was talking about. Reuben was no resistance operative, spy or anything like that. The Germans would never find anything, they were stupid (amongst other reasons) to even consider this.

A few moments later Reuben came to the front door wearing a very expensive black suit, black shoes and carrying a black cane that was more for show than anything else.

The Germans explained what was going on, he protested and let the Germans start their search. They started with the ground floor.

Janet subtly shook her head but as the Germans started their silly searching, her eyes flicked to her

Master and he was concerned.

Janet had known Reuben long enough to know when he wasn't okay. To people who didn't know him very well then they (like the Germans) probably thought he was happy and pleasant.

But he was annoyed, concerned and probably angry.

If there was anything here then Janet just had to help him, but… the strange guests. Janet had never connected it before but what if those strange guests talking about Germany were actually resistant agents?

That made so much sense.

Janet didn't dare let that realisation show at all, but she had to do something.

Clearly Reuben had taken something in for the resistances. It wouldn't be a person because Janet was the only cook and she didn't feed anyone else, and she hadn't seen any food go missing.

It couldn't be that.

Janet seriously doubted Reuben had any secret papers, folders or anything because she cleared his office every other day. There was nothing new there.

Then Janet realised there was one place in the entire house where she wasn't allowed to go. She wasn't allowed to go in the attic, it was never locked or anything but Janet respected Reuben's wishes.

What if something was inside?

Janet subtly looked at the potatoes in her apron and the elegant wooden staircase that would take her (after a while) up to the attic. She had to go and the potatoes would just slow her down.

Equally she couldn't throw them on the ground because that would alert the Germans to what she was doing.

She had to take them with her.

As fast as she could Janet went over to the staircase and started climbing the stairs.

Normally this was an easy job despite Janet's ageing joints. But carrying all the weight of the potatoes wasn't helping her.

"Back half clear!" one of the Germans shouted.

Janet tried to hurry up. She was only halfway up to the first floor and the Germans would be moving to the second floor soon.

She had to hurry.

She kept climbing.

Janet made it to the first floor. She kept on climbing the stairs.

"Ground floor clear!" the Germans shouted.

Then Janet heard the Germans hurrying up the stairs and they immediately dived into searching the first floor.

Janet was sure her legs were about to buckle, the potatoes would be dropped and the Germans would come for her.

They didn't. Janet kept going up the stairs.

Thankfully there were only three floors and the attic in the house, but that gave Janet little comfort.

Janet made it to the second floor. Her heart was racing. She felt tired.

She continued.

"First floor cleared!"

Again the Germans raced up the stairs behind her. The second floor was the largest. It would hopefully take the longest to search.

Janet forced herself to go on. She wasn't sure how much longer she could carry the potatoes.

She made it to the third floor and she couldn't hold this many potatoes anymore. She had to waste valuable time by diving into Reuben's bedroom quickly.

Thankfully she hadn't collected the lunch plates on his desk yet. She placed some potatoes on there.

She hurried out again and went up to the attic. Janet felt so much better now without the extra kilogram or two.

When she got to the top of the stairs there was a very large brown door with a sticky handle that Janet had to try and open. The problem was the potatoes kept her hands busy.

Janet carefully tried to open the door with four fingers. It wasn't moving.

Janet had to ever, ever so carefully take the two corners of her apron that formed the made-shift bag and hold them in one hand. Giving her a hand free to open the door.

She tried with her free hand. It wasn't moving.

She pushed it.

A potato fell out. Rolling down the stairs.

Janet froze. Fears of being captured, sent to

prison and executed gripped her.

The potato rolled into Reuben's bedroom.

Janet tried to open it again. The door opened and Janet went straight inside.

Considering how big the tiny little attic looked, it was rather unimpressive as it was no bigger than ten foot by ten foot, it was covered in dust and there was only a desk by the circular window.

But Janet hated how cold and dark it was up here, she had thought she had heard a strange tapping sound coming from here some nights. Until now she hadn't given it much thought.

Janet went over to the desk and noticed the dust and the darkness had almost hidden a very large suitcase. She popped it open and gasped when she saw a wireless radio transmitter like the resistance used.

She had no clue what the different pieces did, she had just heard this was what they looked like with their little tappy-things, screens and the rest.

She had to get rid of this thing for Reuben before the Germans found it. Janet didn't know how.

Then Janet had an idea. A few years ago she had helped the old cleaner move a large wooden chest up here before the break out of the war and the old cleaner died.

Janet looked around and in a very, very dark corner she saw the very dusty chest. Because of the dust she couldn't tell or remember the colour of the chest, but that didn't matter.

She went over to the chest, opened it and almost cried in delight that the chest was empty.

"Second floor cleared!"

Janet had to hurry. She unloaded most of the potatoes because she wanted to carry the radio out of the attic. No one would suspect she was carrying or hiding it.

With most of the potatoes in the chest, she closed it and went back over to the radio transmitter. She closed the suitcase and put it carefully in her made-shift apron bag.

It was heavy!

To make matters worse, Janet had to get some more potatoes to put on top of the suitcase or it would be easy to tell what it was.

"Third floor clear!"

Janet heard the Germans race up towards her.

Janet raced over to the chest. Grabbed some potatoes. Covered up the suitcase.

She left.

As she calmly walked down the stairs she smiled and nodded to the Germans as they let her past carrying the radio transmitter.

They didn't say a word.

***

An hour later when the Germans had finished researching the house (requiring Janet to hide the transmitter in her wood store), Reuben sat quietly on a very expensive leather chair at the head of a long dining table in the middle of his most decorated room.

Janet had always loved the golden tones, the ocean blue of the wallpaper and the grand art that hung on the walls. She was allowed to sit with Reuben tonight and he was in a very, very good mood as they both sat there with their dinner.

The transmitter was right next to Janet, she had subtly bought it into the dining room when Ruben had started eating his dinner.

Janet lifted it onto the table and passed it over to Reuben.

"Your radio is very heavy Sir," Janet said.

Reuben's face lit up and smiled. Janet had never seen him so happy.

Then Janet quickly told him what she had done with the potatoes and how she had figured it out. Reuben was just shocked.

Reuben stood up and gave Janet a massive hug, something he had never done before, and he even poured her a glass of wine. The last time she had had wine was the night before France's capitulation.

"Thank you," Reuben said. "You really aren't just some simple country woman, are you?"

Janet raised her glass and they cheered each other.

As the night continued, the two loved, smiled and for the first time since the breakout of the war, Janet actually felt good about herself. She had always been worried about where her life had been leading her, but she was actually where she needed to be.

Whilst she would never get involved in her Master's resistance work, she would always protect him and make sure he was safe.

Just like he would do for her.

As the coldness of the December night set in, Janet was glad she was here tonight and not in some cold German prison waiting for her and her Master's execution.

And knowing that was all because of her made her entire year, and she just knew it was going to be a brilliant December and New Year.

INTRODUCTION
Mood/ Genre: Dark Crime

Everyone has their own special version of their perfect Christmas. For some people, their Christmas is made perfect by going to religious services, others love being around their friends and others still love being with family.

Personally my version of a perfect Christmas is, of course, being around my family and loved ones, whilst having plenty of amazing presents and food as well.

But what happens when we all turn this idea on its head?

As a fiction writer, you can get extremely creative with the idea of a perfect Christmas, so definitely check out the next story.

It will definitely grip you and you'll be wondering about what makes a perfect Christmas for a while.

Enjoy!

PERFECT CHRISTMAS

When people ask me what my perfect Christmas is, I always have an answer for them.

My perfect Christmas is hugging with my grandchildren around a roaring warm fire with Christmas songs quietly playing in the ground all whilst I read their favourite stories to them.

That's the sort of grandma I am.

I really love my grandchildren and my own children of course, they're funny, smart and amazing. Meaning I want to be the best grandma I could to them, so when they come round tonight I'm going to make them hot rich coco with little marshmallows and let them stay up as long as they want.

That's the amazing grandma I am.

But when the police showed up and escorted me to their police car, I was not impressed. I mean how dare they interfere with my perfect Christmas.

Sure there's the body of an unfortunate soul on my living room floor, but I need to start making the hot coco for my grandchildren before they turn up.

But as I sit here with my ancient back against the cold hard plastic of the seat, I'm starting to doubt that will ever happen. Now mind you, I honestly wouldn't mind this but the police car smells awful. It smells of cheesy feet and not like the amazing Christmas spices coming from my kitchen.

I also baked my grandchildren a heavenly Christmas cake, but I still need to ice it and marzipan it for them.

Forcing my mind away from the number of problems I was facing (my darling late Jasper always said I needed to be more organised), I turned my attention to the view of my little house outside the car.

There were tall handsome police men and women walking in and out of my house like they owned the place, I wished I had made them cookies now. And I really, really hoped they weren't going to crush any of my winter flowers that lined the small pathway up to my house from the street.

It took me and Jasper years to get those flowers to, well, flower each and every winter like clockwork. Oh and the grandchildren loved them. I hope the police are careful.

With all the watching of the police people almost crush my flowers starting to give me heart problems (at this rate I'm going to miss the time I take my heart meds), I wondered about some of the weird questions the police were asking me.

Now, I don't know why, but why is whenever a body is found in the house of a little old lady do they presume I'm mad or strange?

I have never seen that body before. I only had a quick look before I called the police, I think it was a man, probably young, but I didn't recognise him.

Then you had all the rude police officers

questioning me like I should magically know who it was because they were in my house. It's just typical that the police think like that, well, if they keep interfering with my perfect Christmas plans I'm going to have to say something.

This was outrageous!

A few moments later the car doors opened, slammed shut and the engine started as I saw two policemen sitting in front. The taller man to my left looked at me whilst the other shorter one stared at me in the rearview mirror.

On normal days I'm sure these officers are great people, but for Christ's sake (I'm not sorry for swearing!) why are they interrogating me. I have Christmas cakes to ice and marzipan and I need to make the coco!

After some more moments of silence I decided enough was enough. I am a grandma I have to do what's right for my family.

"Officers, I'm sure this is all a misunderstanding. I need to do things for my grandchildren. You know it's Christmas. You know my family's coming later on. I need to finish everything,"

When I saw the two officers look at each other and smiled, I was shocked. Shocked I tell you. Here I was trying to be there for my family and these two men who probably weren't even old enough to have families were judging me. Judging me of all people!

If I had my handbag with me I would hit them, and yes I am so that sort of old lady.

"Sorry Miss but we need to take you down town,"

I raised my hands to my chest. That poor soul, he must have been murdered or something and the police need my help. That is so nice of them to recognise my importance, you know I actually tried to be a policewoman once, but back then it was so sexist I left. At least I finally get my chance to prove myself.

"Of course officers. Anything you need I'm sure I can help,"

Again the two officers looked at each other, probably agreeing how important I was. Maybe there weren't so bad after all.

***

Maybe I was completely wrong!

I have been stuck in this tiny little interrogation room with ugly black walls, a massive mirror and two chairs for over an hour. What's worse is the entire place smells of horrid cleaning chemicals. What I wouldn't give to be in my wonderfully Christmas scented kitchen right now.

This is stupid.

My grandchildren and my own kids could be standing outside my place in the freezing cold waiting for me. That is just terrible, they must think I'm a terrible grandma, oh I would hate that. I am not a bad grandma.

Taking another horrid breath of those harsh chemicals that made my tongue taste disgusting lemons (I hate lemons with a passion), I noticed how cold the room was.

What did they want? Their people to freeze to death, I wanted to help them with my brilliance, not freeze to death.

Then I saw the two officers from earlier open and close the door behind me and walk around like I was some cheap meal for these two hungry predators.

With the light being so much better than that

awful car, I focused on each officer for a moment. The taller officer was terribly handsome with his dark hair, slim body and perfect jawline. Just like my Jasper was before he died.

But the other one, bless his heart, was pig ugly. No actually, I'm being terribly harsh, he was beautiful to someone. Just not me. With his horse-like face and massive teeth and short hair.

Again not my cup of tea, but I'm sure he'll find someone.

But I have to say the horse faced one did remind me of a neighbour, no sorry, a neighbour's kid that normally checks on me and even does some shopping for me from time to time. Terribly great kid.

In fact I thought he was meant to come round tonight because one of my grandchildren, I know, she's getting on to about eighteen and her brothers are a lot younger. But I still wanted to do the whole perfect Christmas and everything with her, yet I wanted her to meet this neighbour's kid.

You see a grandma always has an eye for love and I think they would make a perfect couple. She's eighteen. He's twenty-one. Perfect.

I must remember to introduce them at some point.

"Miss, are you okay?" Horse-faced asked me.

I shook my head as I realised I must have been in deep thought.

"I'm sorry officer. I was thinking about my grandchildren. Will this take long? I must get back to them,"

The two officers smiled and nodded at each other.

"Miss do you know the man in your kitchen?"

the handsome officer asked.

I shook my head. "No of course not. But I hope he didn't suffer,"

The handsome officer sat down in the chair opposite me.

"I'm afraid that was Mr Tyler Oddlong,"

I gave a friendly smile to the officer but that didn't ring any bells.

Horse-faced knelt down next to me. "According to your neighbours, he came to see you regularly,"

I nodded. "Oh I'm sorry. I just remember him as the neighbour kid,"

Oh damn. That poor kid, I needed him to meet my granddaughter and he was such a good kid, so caring, loving and respectful.

"Did you kill him?" the handsome officer asked.

"I did not!" I shouted.

How the hell could the police think that?

I'm… I'm a good grandma.

I opened my mouth to protest my innocent but my mind went blank and I remembered seeing Tyler earlier. He was smiling, telling me about his Christmas plans then nothing.

"Do you own a rolling pin?" Horse-faced asked.

I nodded as a memory of me gently hitting the palm of my hand with the rolling pin earlier… when Tyler was there.

"I did not kill him," I said, my voice starting to break.

But I couldn't have killed him, I am a great grandma. What grandparents do you know who does so much for their family? I am going to make a perfect Christmas for my kids and my grandchildren.

It will be… a memory of me talking to Tyler

about my granddaughter entered my mind and he wasn't happy. He respectfully declined to meet her, saying he already had a girlfriend, so I protested.

I raised my hands to my face as I realised what happened. I kept pressing Tyler, I wasn't happy, Tyler wanted to leave and I picked up the rolling pin.

But I will have the perfect Christmas.

I simply smiled at the two officers who must have been expecting me to crack or something judging by the look on their faces.

"Please officers. Unless you have any proof I must get back to my house. I have a Christmas cake to ice, marzipan and coco to make,"

The two officers just shook their heads and the handsome officer left.

With Horse-faced following him, he turned back to me before he left and simply said:

"I'm sorry Miss. It isn't Christmas at all. It's March and your family aren't coming this time. Maybe they can visit you in prison,"

When the door slammed shut, I actually smiled as I started to plan my perfect Christmas in prison, because to me the perfect Christmas with me, my children and my grandchildren was the only thing that really mattered.

No matter who got in the way.

AUTHOR OF THE BETTIE ENGLISH PRIVATE MYSTERIES

CONNOR WHITELEY

CRIMINAL RESISTANCE ALLIANCE

A WORLD WAR TWO HISTORICAL MYSTERY SHORT STORY

INTRODUCTION

Mood/ Genre: Light(ish) Historical Fiction

Whilst this might not be the first historical fiction story of the Holiday Extravaganza, this was actually my first time ever writing historical fiction. Because I love the stories about the French resistance and the amazing work they did during world war two, so I decided to write a story about it based on what famous resistance leader Madame Fourcade were in December 1942 in Correze, France.

Personally, my own opinions on historical fiction are very hit and miss, but this is a great world war two story that you really don't want to skip.

And the reason why this story is in the mystery section (or counts as it) of the Extravaganza is because back in world war two being a rebel and doing resistance work was completely illegal. So it was the perfect story to help transport us back in time to continue to the mystery theme of the Extravaganza.

So please continue for a great, enthralling story

about hope, freedom and justice.
Enjoy!

CRIMINAL, RESISTANCE, ALLIANCE
16th December 1942
Correze, France

French Resistance Leader Mary Tencade would never let any of her agents know it but she did love the stunning area of Correze, even if it was the dead of winter. She only wanted them to believe that her sole focus was on what she did best, running Alliance.

She still couldn't believe she was alive, running the largest resistance network in France and she was still free. There had been so many close-calls of late and she hated to know what laid ahead.

But for now Mary just wanted to enjoy the stunning view of Correze from the little window of the abandoned chateau she was in.

It definitely wasn't the best one she had stayed in but it was far from the worse. The chateau hadn't seen any love, attention or respect for decades with its constant ugly layer of dust, dirt and Mary seriously didn't want to consider what else was there.

But it would serve its purpose.

It was the perfect spot for a little break away and hiding spot for a few weeks until she could decide what to do next. It was the most perfect isolated spot in south central France with its wildest and rockiness that made sure very few Germans came here.

They probably thought no sane person or resistance group would dare set up in this most awful place. But Mary didn't agree, its wildness, cold temperatures and isolation made it perfect.

Granted she still had to find somewhere for her radio operative to set up so he could get a clear signal to MI6 in London. But that could definitely wait a little while, she just wanted to enjoy the stunning view out of her bedroom in the chateau.

The wonderfully cold yet fresh air was such a pleasant change from the harsh-smelling air from the German vehicles in the cities and other occupied parts of France that left the taste of foul smoke on her tongue. She would never really be able to stand at a window too much in any other place.

In fact she probably shouldn't be standing here now, so she slowly closed the window shutters, went over to her somewhat soft double bed and just fell onto it.

The world was turning into such a crazy place. More of her agents had been arrested, imprisoned and killed in recent weeks and months. Beautiful, sexy Faerun wasn't back yet and Mary would never admit it to anyone but him, but she did love him.

When she started off in this resistance work with her friend Narave she honestly didn't believe she would be able to do any of this. There were still some days she felt like she couldn't, or she was just kidding herself that her network was important to the war effort.

They were all just amateur spies after all.

Yet there was just something about Faerun with his beautiful body, charisma and… he was just perfect to help run Alliance, work with MI6 and to have as a partner in life. Mary wanted so badly to have him back for Christmas, she knew that might not happen.

The gentle sound of the biting wind blowing outside was so strange to hear after years of constantly tapping of radio transmitters, talking and shouting of her headquarter staff and the inevitable German that was far too commonplace for Mary's liking.

She wanted to change that, but it wouldn't change anytime soon.

Especially with the damn Nazis having invaded Vichy, the so-called independent (more like puppet) free zone of France where the Nazis didn't apparently rule. That happened on the 10th of November, but it just felt like yesterday.

Mary buried herself into her sheets more and more in some pointless attempt to give her some calming comfort. She had loved escaping the police station her and her friends were prisoners in from the help of Anti-Germany Vichy police officers, but she hated that the Germans invaded Vichy the night before.

She would never forget the amazing braveness of those police officers, who wanted to help her and her friends stay alive and support the war effort.

Out of everything going on in the country, Europe and world that was probably what kept her going the most. Mary had always been amazed by the amount of support of people got in the most dire of situations. She knew exactly how lucky she was, most resistant groups didn't get that lucky, but that's what drove her.

She knew how many of those amazing people got caught, imprisoned and executed for helping her and her agents. So she was damn well going to repay the favour and help all of France get free as soon as she could.

That just seemed impossible now with the Vichy police, army and everything else all over France falling into Nazi hands and becoming nothing more than monsters for Hilter.

The number of friends for resistance groups was running out. Fast.

Footsteps came from downstairs.

Mary shot up.

She carefully tried to listen to the voices that were walking about and talking as they did so.

German.

Damn it!

From what Mary could hear there were at least

three Germans downstairs walking about the chateau.

Mary wanted to run, but there was nowhere to go. She had sent her agents out to get some food for the Christmas celebrations and other guests she had coming in a few days.

She was alone.

Mary grabbed the revolver from under her pillow.

She was going hunting.

No Germans were killing her.

***

After carefully tip-toeing down the long, but awfully narrow stone staircase, Mary crouched down and peeked round the corner to spy on her evil visitors. She was surprised how quickly the visitors had managed to make it into the heart of the chateau.

The large meeting room was easily twenty metres long with two large fireplaces carved right into the walls, a long oak table that Mary looked forward to eating round in a few days time was in the middle and a large suitcase was on top.

Mary wanted to rush out and grab the suitcase that was filled with intelligence reports, questionnaires and other things that MI6 had sent her recently.

It might have sounded careless to just leave the suitcase on the table, but Mary had hardly expected to be suddenly attacked by Germans and her staff were only meant to be gone for a little while.

It was a stupid mistake but one she was determined to correct.

The horrible smell of sweat, body odour and dead body made Mary carefully look at the four Germans who were inspecting the meeting room.

They thankfully didn't have the uniform, arrogance or sheer aura of death that came from Gestapo officers, but Mary still didn't want to take any chances.

Then she noticed the dead man on her floor next to one of the fireplaces in the middle of the room. The man was definitely French, probably a blacksmith judging by his rather good muscles, blackened face and the odd burn on his hands.

Mary was hardly impressed that these Germans might not have been spies or secret police but they were definitely killers. They were probably in here trying to find a place to hide the body.

Something she couldn't have anywhere near here.

From reports she had gotten from other resistance networks, having dead bodies about end ever ended well.

One of her friends had killed a German infiltrator and buried him in the garden. The wildlife was drawn to it and it wasn't long until the police turned up and the resistance network fell.

Mary was not letting that happen.

She focused on the four Germans and noticed how they were all carrying the same type of pistol. All Nazi standard issue, they were probably soldiers stationed in a nearby base, but this was Correze, miles away from any type of Nazi base.

These soldiers were probably rogues or something.

And in Mary's experience rogues were just as dangerous, if not more so, than the loyal monsters.

The Germans started muttering to themselves again and Mary noticed a long cast iron fire poker was leaning against the fireplace. It wasn't hard to get to but she would have to be quick.

Mary hardly wanted to use a gun if she could help it because they were far too loud and then any Gestapo units nearby would definitely come running.

She couldn't risk that.

The four Germans walked over to the dead body and stood around him talking and gesturing to the fireplace.

Mary couldn't believe they were actually thinking about burning the body. They clearly didn't know how awful of a smell of that was, it would attract everyone from here to Paris and Marseille.

It was suicide.

Thankfully, Mary knew more than a little German (it helped in coding secret messages and hearing what the enemy were thinking) to get by so she was going to have to risk herself to save her network once again.

She hid her pistol in her back pocket.

"Do you speak French?" she asked, stepping out from the stairs.

The four Germans spun around. Their guns pointed at her.

"We do," the tallest German said.

His short well-styled blond hair and blue eyes almost made Mary laugh. He must have been popular in the military.

"Burning a body will not help you. It causes too much of a smell. A smell that will attract police officers," Mary said calmly.

The Germans sneered at her.

They cocked their pistols.

"What are you? Resistance? British?" the tallest one said.

Mary was almost offended. How dare he think of her as British! As much as she loved the British, MI6 and everything they had given her, she was French to the core. She did all of this so France could be free once more.

She was not British.

"I am a woman who wants to live in peace," Mary said coldly.

The four German people took a step closer and started looking her up and down.

Mary seriously wanted her staff to get back soon.

Mary carefully walked over to the fireplace and made soon the fire poker was within reach if she needed it.

"She's a woman indeed," the tallest man said.

Mary was definitely going to kill him first and foremost.

"Who was the dead man?" Mary asked.

The Germans spat on the corpse behind them.

Mary was tempted to act with them being distracted but that man might be important to someone.

"Just a resistance git who asked too many questions about troop movements. Alliance scum," the tallest man said.

Mary forced herself not to react. The man must have been one of the new recruits that she hadn't met yet.

As much as it pained it about the casual recruitment process of those outside her inner circle, she didn't have an alternative. She still hated losing her agents, even if she didn't know that.

These Germans had to pay.

Mary went for the fire poker. She grabbed it. Swinging it.

The poker smashed into the Germans.

Killing the tallest one instantly.

His blood splashed against the table.

The Germans were shocked. They froze. Mary did not.

She swung it again.

Shattering the skull of another.

Mary rammed it into the head of the third one.

The last German tackled her.

Punching her in the face.

Mary swung the poker again.

It smashed into his chest.

He fell off her.

Mary climbed on top of him.

Smashing the poker through his eye.

A few moments later five men and women ran into the room carrying paper shopping bags, food and weapons. They were shocked to see Mary covered in blood and the corpses around her.

Mary didn't have time to welcome them back. They had to clear up.

"Go back into town carefully," Mary said. "Get some lye. We have bodies to clear up,"

***

25th December 1942

Correze, France

To Mary's utter relief, it had been more than easy for her staff to secretly buy from lye in the local town and as soon as they got back Mary and the others had made sure to dissolve the bodies. A neat trick she had learnt from the British.

As the other sector leaders and agents had turned up and joined her for the Christmas gathering, she had warned them about the bodies and the possible risk they posed to them all.

They had all plotted out escape routes and everyone had agreed that Mary was the most important person who had to escape. Mary loved that dedication but she loved her agents and friends more.

To her very pleasant surprise Faerun had returned on the 17th and that lead to a very pleasurable night and it was wonderful to hear what adventures he had been on in Algiers. And Mary was really looking forward to seeing him again for a little longer.

As Mary sat at the head at the large oak table surrounded by fine food, wine and even finer friends, she just couldn't believe how lucky she was that she was finally able to relax for a little bit and just be a normal person.

A person that could socialise, laugh and just have fun for one day of the year before getting back to constantly running, hiding and intelligence work.

The smell of freshly roasted succulent chicken was intoxicating when combined with the hints of rosemary and thyme that a local shopkeeper had stored from the summer just for them.

And everyone continued their eating, celebrating and Christmas drinking, Mary just smiled at Faerun. The beautiful man who helped her run it all, and the man she truly loved.

It might be the close of one great year, and Mary might have been completely fearful about what was to come in 1943, but she knew she could do anything with the amazing people round the table by her side.

And that simply delighted her.

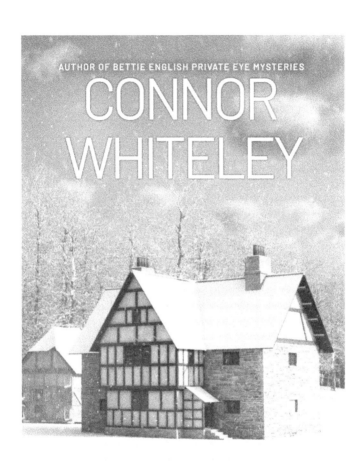

INTRODUCTION

Mood/ Genre: Dark Mystery Crime

Come on!

Did you seriously think we would continue with all this Christmas and Holiday nice rubbish?

Believe me, I was not going to continue all of these happy, joyous stories for too much longer but if memory serves me, this is the last mystery short story of the Extravaganza, so I wanted it to be extra dark.

Also in the UK today is what is known as Boxing Day, which I suppose in next year's Extravaganza I should probably try to do a themed story for this special day in the UK season. But I will not this year. Yet in olden times it was Boxing Day when you opened your presents.

So I really wanted to do today's story to help break up the seasonal joy and happiness of this Extravaganza, and whilst I originally wrote this story to be sent out before Christmas. I realised I really needed a dark story to help us recover from the nonstop joy of the past week.

Please download or turn the page to enjoy this wonderfully dark, moving and criminally good short story about a brother wanting to protect his siblings.

Enjoy!

DARK FARM

Farm Boy Tyler Gray stood on the freezing cold dirt road surrounded by endless fields buried under a thick layer of the whitest of snow that looked like endless blankets veiling the land with his family's farm Tudor-style farmhouse in the middle of the farm.

Tyler continued to stand there in the dirt road as he watched his father's wooden wagon ride off into the distance. His father had said he was going away for a few days in hope of selling some of the last grain, potatoes and chicken that the family had from this year's harvest.

Tyler just hoped his father would make it back in time for Christmas.

The forecast had promised there be another two snowstorms, which for England was a rarity in its own right, so Tyler was seriously starting to doubt if his precious father would come back in time for Christmas.

He couldn't imagine anything worse than being

stuck with his mother, two sisters and little brother for Christmas. His mother was an awful woman, loud, abusive and just foul.

Thankfully she had been okay recently, happy even, but Tyler and his eldest sister Franny knew that would change in an instance.

The only thing Tyler could do now was wait, and if any trouble did come up, he had to be the man of the house now and protect his siblings.

As it was only morning, and a damn cold one at that, Tyler and his siblings had enough chores to do that all of them should be able to avoid their mother for most of the day. Tyler would have liked to just get rid of her entirely but he wasn't sure his father would like that.

As much as Tyler absolutely loved his father for his laughter, kindness and patience. He was as blind as a tree to his wife's cruelness. Tyler had tried to tell him so many times about what his mother had done to his sisters, but his father never believed him.

And every single time that happened it killed Tyler inside. He wanted to protect his sisters, but he was nothing more than a failure in that department.

When Tyler could no longer see his father's wagon, he sadly started to walk back towards the farmhouse. It was a great walk actually, Tyler loved seeing the endless amount of snow that perfectly covered the land.

It was like he was living in a winter wonderland.

After a few minutes, Tyler walked past the little

outhouses, wooden storage sheds and a rather tall windmill that was meant to make power for the farm, but it had been broken for years.

Next year Tyler was going to fix it up, no matter how much that mother of his protested. She didn't get a voice in how the farm was run.

Tyler went to the large wooden door in the Tudor-style farmhouse that led to the kitchen. Tyler smiled and was filled with relief at the sight of the multiple pieces of string attached to the door were still intact.

The string was one of the most important things on the farm in his opinion. It allowed them to survive and navigate the farm despite how bad the storm was.

The string had saved Tyler's life more than once.

Tyler went into the large brown kitchen with its little-brown worktops lining the outside, the large gas stove and sink against the far edge of the kitchen, and to Tyler's complete surprise his youngest brother and sister were sitting round the wooden table smiling, laughing and eating a freshly cooked breakfast.

It smelt amazing with its fresh hints of sausages, bacon and eggs that filled the entire kitchen. It smelt like a home filled with love, respect and admiration. Tyler was definitely going to have to thank Fanny for cooking the breakfast for them.

"Tyler!" his mother shouted as her overweight body stomped across the kitchen and hugged him.

Tyler was filled with horror at the idea of his mother loving him and being in a good mood. Her breath stunk of whiskey. His father had promised Tyler before he left that all the whiskey was gone but clearly his mother had hidden more bottles somewhere.

Tyler gave his mother a quick kiss on the forehead, smiled and then carefully went over to Fanny who was standing in the kitchen doorway that led into the living room at the other end of the kitchen near the stove.

Tyler was impressed to see Fanny in her jeans, red and green t-shirt and jumper. She looked good, but Tyler could see how worried she was about the breakfast and everything.

This wasn't going to end well.

They both knew that.

The only problem with being the oldest at 20 of the family was that Tyler just felt like everything was down to him these days. It didn't matter that Fanny was 18, his youngest sister was 14 and his brother was 12.

Tyler was still nervous as hell because of it.

As much as Tyler wanted to stay and watch the breakfast and jump in if he was needed. He did have jobs to do and if he was going from past experience, him just being there and watching built-up tensions.

So if he left he might be doing everyone a favour.

The sound of the wind howling outside made Tyler fold his arms. There was a snowstorm now.

Tyler went over to his foul mother and hugged her.

"Thanks for doing this mum," he said.

His mother smiled. "Course dear. Happy to. Are you going to work today?"

"Yea, dad wanted me to check some of the outhouses," Tyler said.

His mother kissed and hugged him and then smiled.

"You wrap up warm little one. Stay safe," she said.

Tyler smiled and kissed her again on the head then he put on his massively coat, (fake) fur-lined boots and went outside.

As Tyler was surprised at the snowstorm was as heavy as it was, he couldn't see the outhouses, the broken windmill or the fields anymore. They were all covered in a shroud of snow, but Tyler wasn't going to the outhouses. He wanted to check on the broken windmill.

He was now starting to believe that if he could repair it before his father got home then it would be a perfect Christmas present to the whole family on the big day.

Tyler found the piece of string that led to the windmill and he followed it carefully. He didn't risk falling over in case he pulled and broke the string. Then he would be a dead man.

But Tyler wasn't going to deny that his mother's sweet nature this morning wasn't concerning him. It was great when she was like that, and that was why Tyler always made sure he got enough love and attention to last him until his mother was like that again (in another year).

Yet when she did turn, she was always so horrible, foul and even worse than usual. Tyler didn't want to be out for too long, just in case his mother did turn on them.

After a few minutes of struggling through the snow, Tyler walked into the freezing cold wooden door of the broken windmill. He couldn't even see the door that was how bad the storm was, and he couldn't even hear himself think. The howling was so bad.

Tyler forced open the door to the windmill and shot inside.

The smell of whiskey, bourbon and stale beer was overwhelming. And when Tyler really focused on the large box room after recovering from the shock of the warmer room, he was disgusted at the amount of empty and full whiskey bottles he saw.

No one wonder his mother had protested so much to him coming in here. This was where she was hiding everything she shouldn't have in the first place.

Tyler wanted to smash them all up, but that would probably just make things worse.

She might think that one of his sisters or young brother came in here and smashed them. She might attack, harm and abuse them like she normally did.

No.

Tyler couldn't do anything about the bottles until his father was bad safe and sound. Then Tyler would smash the bottles (or steal them and sell them in the town for a bit of money). Then if his mother turned abusive, his father could finally see.

After about an hour of checking out the windmill, its upper floors and its electricals, Tyler just laughed at himself for even thinking he could do it alone in a few days.

It was a much larger job than that but he had a pretty good idea about what to do, so he could tell his father his plan and they could hopefully do it together.

They would both love that.

Tyler went back out of the windmill, grabbed the string and went back to the kitchen door. When he went inside, the smell of sausages, bacon and eggs was long gone, and Tyler just felt like you could cut the tension with a knife.

Tyler quietly took off his boots and coat and went into the large living room, with its massive Christmas tree, red sofas and roaring fireplace where Fanny was holding the two youngest children who were screaming and crying their eyes out.

Tyler was just furious. He wanted to shout and demand an explanation from his mother, but then he heard a massive door slam.

That was exactly what his mother always did as soon as he came in. She always locked herself away in her room.

Tyler went over to Fanny and lovingly took his little brother from her, cradling him in his arms.

"What happened?" Tyler asked quietly.

Fanny shrugged. "These two asked about going out to build a snowman. She flipped out and punched them both,"

Tyler just held his brother tight. There was no reason to hurt them, all she needed to do was tell them it wasn't safe with the storm.

Tyler kept hugging his brother and just wished his mother was no longer about. But he was starting to get worried about his father, did he make it to town before the storm?

Was he going to make it back for the big day?

Was he ever coming back?

Fanny moved closer to Tyler and they all just sat there in silence, comforting and supporting each other. Tyler had always known Fanny was a great caring mother, and her own kids when she was older were going to be extremely lucky.

But Tyler just wanted his father to hurry up and return.

***

For the rest of the day, Tyler and Fanny and the two youngest children laughed, sang and told stories in the living room next to the roaring fire. It was the most fun Tyler had had for ages, it was amazing what having real family time could do for a person.

Then as the day got late, Tyler and Fanny went into their bedrooms and bought out the duvets and pillows so they could all sleep in front of the protective warmth of the fire tonight.

They had all been sleeping for hours when it struck midnight and Tyler heard someone moving about the house. He carefully looked up from his makeshift bed and saw the bulk of his mother slip into the kitchen.

Tyler then heard the kitchen door open.

As much as he wanted to talk to his mother, he knew that wouldn't change anything.

Tyler silently got up, he didn't bother to put on any of his warm clothing. He just opened the door, felt the pieces of string that shot off from the house until he felt a piece tighter than the others.

He had to force his very cold self not to laugh in the slightest when he knew his mother was going to the windmill. The storm at this point was the worse Tyler had ever seen, he couldn't even see his hand that was only about twenty centimetres away.

Tyler untied the string. It fell to the floor. Then Tyler locked the kitchen for good measure.

His mother was going to freeze to death.

Thankfully.

***

After making a wonderfully light, refreshing breakfast of some preserved fruits and homemade yoghurt for the young ones, Tyler and Fanny both stood at the little kitchen window and stared at the perfectly calm morning.

The sun was shining more than Tyler had seen in months, even the temperature was surprisingly pleasant, and right in the middle of the farm and windmill was a frozen and very dead woman.

Their mother was finally dead and the abuse could stop.

Tyler would never tell his family what he did, and he just knew they didn't care but Fanny just hugged him so tight.

"Thank you," she whispered.

Tyler just shrugged. At the end of the day, Tyler was just doing what he thought was right for himself, his family and his father. But they were all free now to enjoy life without the constant threat of her abuse.

"You know she was scared of you," Fanny said.

Tyler just smiled. It would explain why she never came out of her room after she abused his siblings, and maybe she was right to be scared of him. He did, after all, kill her.

But she never should have abused his family in the first place.

The sound of crunching snow made all four siblings race to put on their coats and boots and they ran out of the farmhouse.

Their daddy was home.

Tyler just felt so pleased that his father was back safe and sound, and as he climbed down from his wagon and petted the horse. He saw the body of his wife, and looked at Tyler.

Tyler felt his heart jump to his throat. Was his father about to shout and disown him?

Was his father about to hit him?

Was his father about to leave them all forever?

Instead his father just gave him a sad smile when he saw the two massive bruises on the youngest siblings' faces, and he hugged Tyler.

"I'm so sorry," his father said.

Tyler just hugged him back tight because his father wasn't mad at him or his siblings. He loved them because he was a good father, a damn good one.

And with Christmas in just a few days, Tyler couldn't wait to spend it with his real family. His siblings and father that actually loved, cared and wanted the best for each other.

Because today wasn't a sad day. It was a day that marked the beginning of a new start for all of them, the start of being free from an abuser and Tyler was really, really looking forward to how great that was going to feel.

INTRODUCTION
Mood/ Genre: Light Private Eye Mystery

After Christmas and the big feast, there can occasionally (always) be tons of food leftover, leaving some with a few different options depending on the family. You could wrap up the food and eat it over the next few days, you could bin it (please don't do that) or you could reuse it in some creative way.

Personally, me and my family tend to save the leftovers after Christmas day dinner and pick at it for the rest of Christmas Day before dessert.

Then as there is always plenty of food leftover including desserts, we save it and reuse it on my mum's birthday which is a few days after Christmas and then we try and use it all up before it goes off.

So when I was asked to submit a short story to a Christmas anthology based on a Made-Up Holiday, I knew that I had to create a holiday based on all this leftover food.

Of course, I won't spoil the story in the slightest,

but as you read our final (and probably best) Bettie English short story of the Holiday Extravaganza. I can promise you, you're in for a very interesting, enthralling mystery centred around leftover food.

And if you want to read more about the Bettie English's mysteries, then you will love the first full-length book in the series *A Very Private Woman* available from all major booksellers in electronic and paper from March 2023.

Enjoy!

GREAT GIVE AWAY

Bettie English, Private Eye, loved her mother's birthday. It was always an amazing day filled with laughter, love and plenty of tasty food. But as she stood on the pavement of a long road with little houses lining each side of it, she was hardly impressed.

She had told her boyfriend, who was currently bent over the engine of her red car, to take a right then a left. That wasn't hard. It was easy, she had done it hundreds of times and her sister had done it drunk even more times.

But no. Her boyfriend Detective Graham had to take left then right, leading them to this God forsaken little road (Street?) with pretty little houses far away from her mother's house and then the car broken down.

Bettie was not impressed!

She didn't even know if Graham knew anything about cars. He was a detective, he was amazing at his job, but as she had learnt way too many times recently if she told him to put his mind to anything else, he was sexy and hot as hell, but next to useless.

Bettie had to admit watching Graham in his tight jeans, white shirt and blue shoes bend over her car was probably the only upside of the situation. Yet Bettie was starting to realise that they were going to be stuck here for a while and she hoped, prayed, whatever-ed that her mother's birthday cake wasn't going to spoil.

Granted it was cold enough. Late December was always cold in southeast England and all the little houses were covered in a thin layer of ice, frost and even a little snow, but Bettie didn't like how her breath condensed into long columns of vapour.

The smell of wonderfully warming spices filled the air and Bettie loved those smells as she remembered the buttery, luxurious mince pies she had eaten all over Christmas along with the fruity, boozy cake and yule logs. It really had been the perfect Christmas with her family and now she wanted to top it off with the perfect birthday for her mother, but that clearly wasn't going to happen within the next hour.

The sound of panicked voices in the distance made Bettie wonder what was going on. It was clear the voices were coming from further down the street, and considering Bettie had nothing better to do and Graham would never call the breakdown services, she had no other choice than to check out the sound.

And it meant Graham wouldn't be able to spring up the conversation of having kids on her again, like he had accidentally done that morning.

A conversation she really didn't want today. Especially as her mother was going to ask about it a thousand times already.

"Gra, I'm going down the street to check down

the sounds. Be back soon. Love you," Bettie said, walking down the street.

"Love you too Bet," Graham said.

Bettie actually looked at the houses as she went down the street, they were more beautiful than her quick glance had showed her earlier. Each house still had up their wide range of Christmas lights in all their different stunning colours. They were rather beautiful. Each one could probably be described as an art piece with how each house had shaped, decorated and sequenced their lights.

But why were the lights on at nine o'clock in the morning? It was hardly dark.

"The Gift is stolen!"

Bettie stared at the man who kept shouting the same thing over and over. She wasn't sure what to make of the man, he wasn't very tall, but his (hideously) bright Christmas jumper and trousers spoke volumes.

"Bettie English, Private Eye, can I help you?" she asked.

"Oh yes, you can," the man turned towards the rest of the street. "Everyone! The Great Give Away is saved!"

Bettie really didn't understand what was going on. At this rate she'll have to charge a confusion fee to these people.

As more and more people walked out of their houses towards Bettie, she couldn't believe how they all looked so different. Each person was a different height, weight and class. That alone was different from the rest of England.

"Miss? Who are you?" a little old lady said pulling on Bettie's arm.

Bettie introduced herself and wasn't sure what to make of the little old lady as her face lit up like a Christmas tree.

"Miss, the Great Give Away is lost without you?"

Now Bettie wished she had had that second mug of coffee like Graham had wanted her to. Damn him for being right!

"Sorry. What is the Great Give Away?" Bettie asked.

Everyone in the street gasped and looked at horror at Bettie.

"It's the most amazing time of the year!" everyone shouted.

The little old lady placed a cold hand on Bettie's shoulder.

"Miss. Every year on this day, we Give Away all our Christmas leftovers to the homeless so they may get fed through the New Year after our Christmas joy,"

That was a rather good idea actually, Bettie had never thought of that beforc. It made perfect sense and she was a bit surprised that no one else had thought of it. Everyone always bought too much at Christmas (that alone was disgusting) and everyone just threw it away (including her), but giving it to the homeless and less fortunate, now that was an excellent idea.

But the idea of someone stealing it was monstrous. Who in their right mind would steal from such a great idea?

It was probably as far from the Christmas spirit that you could get. Especially given the entire idea of St Nick and Father Christmas was to give the poor presents and help others. This theft was flat outrageous!

Bettie had to find out who did it.

The little old lady and everyone else grabbed Bettie and pulled her further down the street.

Bettie tried to resist but she just went along with it in the end.

Then the crowd pushed her in front of a large metal cage with red, pink and green tinsel covering it. But there was one very disturbing thing that caught Bettie's eyes, where a presumably large metal padlock should have been, there was only bend twisted metal.

"Is this where you stored the leftovers?" Bettie asked.

Another massive gasp from the crowd.

The little old lady gestured for the crowd to go away and leave her and Bettie alone.

"Miss. I'm sorry about that. For them The Great Give Away is the highlight of the year, they believe everyone should do it,"

"I do agree. Tell me what happened?"

"I run the street Miss. I own most of it and now walk up and down every morning and evening if my old body allows me. I walked past this morning to see the food was gone,"

"Was it there last night?" Bettie asked.

"Oh yes Miss. I bought some leftover… I mean The Gift of My Husband's Christmas Cake to donate,"

Bettie smiled. "It's okay. Say whatever you want to me, I won't get offended,"

"Thank you Miss,"

Bettie knelt down on the cold ground, looking at the twisted metal. It was clear that the lock had been forced off but that wasn't what bothered Bettie so much.

Now she was on the ground, Bettie saw stains of coffee, tea and syrups, but they were all going in the direction of the back of the cage. Not the front.

Bettie would have imagined if the thief had broken off the lock, then they would have pulled all the goods and leftovers through the front and presumably onto whatever they were using to transport the food away.

In fact the ground was cold, perfectly soft and perfectly intact. There were no impressions of feet or wheelbarrow marks or anything else that would suggest someone had been standing here weighted down with all the leftovers.

Something wasn't right here.

Bettie went round to the back of the metal cage.

"Here," Bettie said.

"What Miss?"

Bettie just pointed to the deep marks and the stains of tea, coffee and syrups in the mud.

"Oh Miss!" the little old lady said, her voice panicked.

Bettie tapped the back of the metal cage a few times and watched it vibrate, hum and eventually fall off.

"Someone must have carefully cut off the back part, stole the leftovers and twisted the lock off to make you think that was how the theft happened,"

"Oh dear Miss, oh dear. What will I do?"

Bettie stood up and placed a gentle hand on the old lady.

"Relax. It will be okay. I will find your leftovers for you. But can I ask a favour?"

"Anything Miss!"

Bettie smiled. "There's a little red car up the street with a hot man failing to fix my engine. Do you have a mechanic on the street please?"

Again the old lady's eyes lit up and she simply walked away.

Bettie had no idea if that meant they had a mechanic, or if the old lady had simply gone off to check out Graham. It sounded silly, but in Bettie's past experience the older women of the world did enjoy his looks. Thankfully she was younger than him by a few years.

Bettie knelt down next to the marks in the soft mud. They didn't look right or what she had seen from other thefts in her years as a private eye.

The marks were too narrow to be car wheels and she doubted anyone could get a car on the soft mud and get it off again without the car spinning out. Then again the marks were still too large to belong to a wheelbarrow.

And judging by the size of the metal cage and the odd marks of rice pudding on the top of it, Bettie was sure the cage had been stuffed full.

But the marks did go away from the metal cage towards one of the little houses who had a large brown fence.

Bettie went up to the fence and strangely enough the marks seemed to go straight under the fence like it wasn't there.

Maybe it hadn't?

Jumping out Bettie grabbed onto the top of the fence and pulled herself up, she'd forgotten how tough climbing was. In the new year she had to get back to the gym and do weight training, forget cardio, she had to do the weights!

Over the fence, Bettie didn't like the plainness of the little garden that she was looking at. All the garden had in it was a child's swing, a sandpit and a bed of half-dead flowers.

It all looked so plain and unloved. Unlike her garden, this one didn't scream love, nature or beauty. It looked like some half-ass attempt to make a garden fit for a family.

But the marks weren't in the garden.

"Can I help ya?" a woman said.

Bettie dropped down from the fence.

The woman in front of her was hardly a looker with her long twisted hair, short stocky body and black teeth, but Bettie had dealt with worse looking people.

"Yes actually. Did you-"

"Leave woman. I donna have time for ya. Go away and don't come back," the woman said starting to leave.

"Does your kid want a new bike?" Bettie said, randomly.

The woman stopped. "Go away. My kid don't want anything from a posh snob like you. Now leave,"

"How about some Gifts from The Great Give Away?"

The woman hissed at Bettie as she almost went into her house.

"Those snobs donna give me any. I might be poor, but I gotten a house. Now leave. I don't want ya charity,"

The door slammed shut and Bettie wasn't sure what to make of it. The woman was clearly annoyed at the street, snobs that lived here (even though Bettie had met snobs and these people weren't ones) and hated the Great Give Away.

But the woman had seen contempt at least a little bit to live her life how she wanted, Bettie doubted the woman wanted to do any harm to the world.

Bettie went over to the woman's door and pushed a twenty-pound note through the letterbox. At least the woman might be able to buy herself and her kids some food and maybe a nice treat with it.

The sound of a bike's bell made Bettie look at the street as she saw two young children ride around.

She still didn't know if she wanted kids, Graham definitely did, but he was a detective, she was a private eye. Full time jobs and lifestyles that didn't allow for kids, but she still had time to find out, if that's what she wanted.

Then Bettie looked at the tyres on the bikes, they were narrow, smaller than a car and wheelbarrow. They might be able to make the marks in the soft mud.

Bettie went over to the side of the road and knelt down.

"Kids," Bettie said, waving them over.

"Mum said don't talk to strangers!" one of the kids said, he was probably about ten.

Bettie rolled her eyes. "I'm a friend of the… little old lady, owns some of the houses,"

She had no idea if they would know who she was talking about.

"Mrs Birchwood!" the younger kid shouted, he was certainly six years old.

The ten year old kid got off his bike and walked over to Bettie, keeping at least three metres between himself and her. Very clever, Bettie was going to have to remember that if she had kids. Three metres was more than enough space to run away if she wanted to kidnap him.

Of course she didn't, but still.

"Are you two the only ones with bikes in the street?" Bettie asked.

"Na. Jonny boy has a big bikey for big boys,"

"Has he ride a lot?"

"Ya. Saw him riding last night after Birchwood did her walky. I donna think she was gotten make it back home, I was gonna ride her home but mum said no,"

Bettie only just realised that there was something amazing about young children. They always wanted to love, help and support others no matter what, if she was going to have kids, she had to teach them that. And then make sure they didn't lose it when they grew up.

"That's very good of you. Well done. Now where do I find this Jonny Boy?"

The kid shrugged, jumped on his bike and they both rode off again.

***

When Bettie returned to her little red car she was expecting to stare at her beautiful Graham bent over the engine failing to fix it. Instead she found the little old lady bend over and hammering away at the engine.

The wonderful smell of the warming Christmas spices filled the air as Bettie went up to Graham who had a few dark smudges on his white shirt and tight jeans, but he was still the sexy, most beautiful man Bettie had ever seen.

"At least you tried," Bettie said, rubbing

Graham's muscular shoulder.

"You clearly didn't trust me," Graham said, pretending to hit her cheek.

The little old lady climbed down to the ground and out of the car and turned to Bettie.

"Miss, your car should be working again in no time. Cars advanced a lot since the war but it will work,"

"You worked in the war?" Bettie asked, doubting the old lady was old enough to serve during World War Two.

"Oh no Miss, me dad served and I was born later. He taught me a lot about cars, trucks and planes from the war. I was quite the fixer in the neighbourhood. Have you found the Great Give Away?"

"The Great Give Away?" Graham asked.

Bettie just waved Graham silent.

"That's why I came to find you. One, thank you for your father's service. Two, who is Jonny Boy?"

The Little Old Lady shrugged.

"I met two kids who called him that and said he had a bike for big boys. Maybe he's an older kid or a young adult?" Bettie said.

"Oh! Miss, you mean Jonathan Bodie,"

Now Bettie shrugged. She didn't know anyone on the street, and yet this woman was acting like Bettie was a local.

"Um yes. Where is he?" Bettie asked.

The little old lady started to walk down the street.

"Come on Miss English. I'm waiting for a part from my garage. My Husband will find it soon. I'll show you where he lives,"

Bettie gestured Graham to follow and they both

followed the little old lady down the street. Even with the sun high in the sky, Bettie couldn't believe how cold and dark it was, but that was the strange thing about English weather, it never seemed natural.

The days were meant to get brighter after the Winter Solstice but they seemed to be getting darker and darker and darker, and even at ten O'clock it wasn't what Bettie would call bright.

But the strangeness of the English weather was something she loved about it though.

After a few more minutes of walking down the street, the little old lady pointed to a bright red and green door with a large wreath on it.

Bettie went up to it and knocked three times.

"Mr Bodie," Bettie said.

A tall man opened the door and Bettie was immediately taken by the amount of aftershave he was wearing, she had to focus on not passing out of its strength. It wasn't even a nice aftershave, not like the earthy, sexy one Graham was wearing.

"Merry Christmas!" Jonathan Bodie said in a happy manly voice.

"Um, Happy Christmas. Did you ride your bike last night?" Bettie asked.

She wanted to start off easy and at least place him at the scene of the crime before outright accusing him. Yet the man seemed too happy and filled with the Christmas spirit to want to steal and ruin the Christmas Season for others.

"Oh Yes, I love cycling. It's wonderful. Especially seeing all the amazing lights. Have you seen them! Have you seen them!"

Bettie nodded. "They are wonderful. Did you go to the Give Away… cage last night?"

Bodie's expression changed to a solid frown and his eyes flicked towards Graham.

Bettie clicked her fingers at him. "Yes he is a cop. But I'm not. Confess to me and nothing can happen to you. I won't tell him, you have my word,"

Bodie's eyes flicked between Bettie and Graham and a few times at the little old lady.

"The homeless peeps can't have the food. We need it. Well, my daughter's charity needs it,"

Bettie shook her head. "You're telling me. You stole the food for the good of others?"

Bodie's eyes widened and he frantically nodded.

Bettie looked at Graham and the little old lady.

"We're going to need a cup of tea for this one," she said.

"Bodie, let the Miss and Graham come in," the little old lady said.

Bettie looked at Bodie who slowly nodded his head and stepped out of the way.

***

The living room of Bodie's house was a lot nicer than Bettie had imagined. She loved his bright blue three seat sofa, chair opposite it and coffee table in the middle.

The living room was definitely small and minimalist but Bodie had managed to make it comforting and cozy and rather lovely despite its size.

There were a few pictures of his wife and presumably his three children on the walls and seeing all those pictures and the happiness of the family made Bettie just stare at Graham.

He was happy, sexy and beautiful, a perfect man who would make an amazing dad. Then she would make a great mother she supposed, Bettie loved her nephew Sean like her own child and had raised him (sometimes) a lot more than his own parents.

So maybe she could have children.

"Please sit down," Bodie said gesturing towards the three seat sofa as he sat down on the chair opposite them.

Bettie sat down. "Your daughter works for a charity?"

Bodie looked at the little old lady. "I'm sorry Margaret. I didn't mean to steal it. My daughter… my daughter just wanted a little help,"

"It's fine deary. But why didn't you just ask?"

Bodie looked to the ground. "I was embarrassed,"

"What is the charity?" Bettie asked.

"It's brilliant Miss. I love it. It's a new charity that helps the homeless, vulnerable youths and even the elderly,"

"My daughter wanted a little help. I didn't want the Great Give Away to only go to one type of person," Bodie said.

Bettie could agree with that. Her nephew could have been one of the vulnerable youths if her (idiot) of a brother-in-law had kicked him out when her nephew said he was gay. Sure Sean would have been homeless but he was still a vulnerable youth, it wasn't fair that he wouldn't necessarily benefit from the Great Give Away, just because he was young.

And most homeless in the area were older.

Bettie leant forward. "Graham I don't think there's a crime here if we reach an agreement,"

Graham smiled and Bettie loved that sexy movie star smile.

"Me either Bet, but what sort of agreement?"

Graham said.

"Well why don't you Mr Bodie and… Margaret agree to support your daughter's charity with the Great Give Away so she can help even more people?"

Both Bodie and Margaret looked at each other and smiled.

"Oh Miss that is a wonderful idea. That way we can all help the homeless, young and the elderly! That is marvellous!"

Bodie nodded too and judging by his face he was trying to hold back some tears.

Bettie stood up and looked at Bodie. "Just to check I presume the food is all in the garage safe and sound,"

Bodie nodded.

"Good. We will leave you both to sort out the details," Bettie said with a smile.

Graham started to head out the door and Bettie went to follow him when Margaret grabbed her arm.

"Thank you Miss! Thank you. You've saved the Great Give Away. What do I owe you?"

Judging by the look on Graham's face as he looked outside, her car was fixed and there was something wonderful about the little street.

Unlike the normal streets of southeast England, this one actually had soul, character and love in it. All these people no matter their background all loved each other in their own unique ways and wanted to help others. Hence the Great Give Away, Bettie wasn't going to charge people who wanted to help out others and help make the world a better place.

"Nothing," Bettie said smiling and walking out of the house. "Merry Great Give Away and A Happy New Year,"

Bettie heard Margaret and Bodie laugh, talk and being happy as she left, and her and Graham walked back up the street towards her car that was working perfectly.

There was a little old man walking away covered in oil and black smudges. He had to be Margaret's husband and the one who fixed the car properly.

She really wished everyone on the street, in England and the rest of the world had a great day and in some small way benefited from the Great Give Away. Because for some reason, a reason even Bettie didn't understand, she truly believed that every little act of kindness helped to make the world a better place.

Bettie wrapped her arm around Graham's waist and buried her face into his shoulder.

"When we get home tonight, we're so doing two things," Bettie said.

"What?"

"We're going to empty the house of the leftovers and take it down to the food bank,"

Graham smile and nodded at that.

Bettie stopped and pulled Graham close. "And we're going to make a baby,"

Graham's face lit up, they kissed and Bettie loved the soft feeling of his lips.

"Merry Great Give Away Bet,"

As Bettie pressed her lips against his, the entire world felt right as she had saved a made-up holiday for people, helped a charity and now she was going to be something she never thought she had wanted.

A mother.

And she had done that all before Eleven O'clock in the morning. A great, brilliant, perfect start to an amazing day.

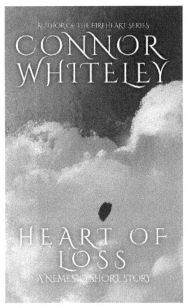

GET YOUR FREE AND EXCLUSIVE SHORT STORY NOW! LEARN ABOUT NEMESIO'S PAST!

https://www.subscribepage.com/fireheart

About the author:

Connor Whiteley is the author of over 60 books in the sci-fi fantasy, nonfiction psychology and books for writer's genre and he is a Human Branding Speaker and Consultant.

He is a passionate warhammer 40,000 reader, psychology student and author.

Who narrates his own audiobooks and he hosts The Psychology World Podcast.

All whilst studying Psychology at the University of Kent, England.

Also, he was a former Explorer Scout where he gave a speech to the Maltese President in August 2018 and he attended Prince Charles' 70th Birthday Party at Buckingham Palace in May 2018.

Plus, he is a self-confessed coffee lover!

More From The Holiday Extravaganza:

Criminal Christmas:
Crime, Christmas, Closet
Protecting Christmas
Christmas Thief
Christmas, Crime, letter
Private Eye, Convention and Christmas
Cheater At Dinner
Perfect Christmas
Salvation In The Maid
Criminal, Resistance, Alliance
Dark Farm
Great Give Away

Sweet Christmas
Lights, Love, Christmas
Journalist, Zookeeper, Love
Young Romantic Hearts
Love In The Newspaper
Holiday, Burnout, Love
Homeless, Charity, Love
Cold December Night
Driving Home For Love
Love At The Winter Wedding
Fireworks, New Year, Love
Loving In The New Year Tourist

Fantastical Christmas:
Magic That Binds
One Final Christmas
Author's Christmas Problems
Last Winter Dragon Egg
A Sacrifice For Saturnalia
Soulcaster
Weird First Christmas
All Feast
Solstice Guardian
Wheel of Years
Repent

OTHER SHORT STORIES BY CONNOR WHITELEY

Mystery Short Stories:
Poison In The Candy Cane
Christmas Innocence
You Better Watch Out
Christmas Theft
Trouble In Christmas
Smell of The Lake
Problem In A Car
Theft, Past and Team
Embezzler In The Room
A Strange Way To Go
A Horrible Way To Go
Ann Awful Way To Go
An Old Way To Go
A Fishy Way To Go
A Pointy Way To Go
A High Way To Go
A Fiery Way To Go
A Glassy Way To Go
A Chocolatey Way To Go
Kendra Detective Mystery Collection Volume 1
Kendra Detective Mystery Collection Volume 2
Stealing A Chance At Freedom
Glassblowing and Death
Theft of Independence
Cookie Thief
Marble Thief
Book Thief

Art Thief
Mated At The Morgue
The Big Five Whoopee Moments
Stealing An Election
Mystery Short Story Collection Volume 1
Mystery Short Story Collection Volume 2

Science Fiction Short Stories:
The First Rememberer
Life of A Rememberer
System of Wonder
Lifesaver
Remarkable Way She Died
The Interrogation of Annabella Stormic
Blade of The Emperor
Arbiter's Truth
Computation of Battle
Old One's Wrath
Puppets and Masters
Ship of Plague
Interrogation
Edge of Failure
One Way Choice
Acceptable Losses
Balance of Power
Good Idea At The Time
Escape Plan
Escape In The Hesitation
Inspiration In Need
Singing Warriors

Knowledge is Power
Killer of Polluters
Climate of Death
The Family Mailing Affair
Defining Criminality
The Martian Affair
A Cheating Affair
The Little Café Affair
Mountain of Death
Prisoner's Fight
Claws of Death
Bitter Air
Honey Hunt
Blade On A Train

<u>Fantasy Short Stories:</u>
City of Snow
City of Light
City of Vengeance
Dragons, Goats and Kingdom
Smog The Pathetic Dragon
Don't Go In The Shed
The Tomato Saver
The Remarkable Way She Died
The Bloodied Rose
Asmodia's Wrath
Heart of A Killer
Emissary of Blood
Dragon Coins
Dragon Tea

Dragon Rider
Sacrifice of the Soul
Heart of The Flesheater
Heart of The Regent
Heart of The Standing
Feline of The Lost
Heart of The Story
City of Fire
Awaiting Death

Other books by Connor Whiteley:

Bettie English Private Eye Series
A Very Private Woman
The Russian Case
A Very Urgent Matter
A Case Most Personal
Trains, Scots and Private Eyes
The Federation Protects

The Fireheart Fantasy Series
Heart of Fire
Heart of Lies
Heart of Prophecy
Heart of Bones
Heart of Fate

City of Assassins (Urban Fantasy)
City of Death
City of Marytrs
City of Pleasure
City of Power

Agents of The Emperor
Return of The Ancient Ones
Vigilance
Angels of Fire
Kingmaker

The Garro Series- Fantasy/Sci-fi
GARRO: GALAXY'S END
GARRO: RISE OF THE ORDER
GARRO: END TIMES
GARRO: SHORT STORIES
GARRO: COLLECTION
GARRO: HERESY
GARRO: FAITHLESS
GARRO: DESTROYER OF WORLDS
GARRO: COLLECTIONS BOOK 4-6
GARRO: MISTRESS OF BLOOD
GARRO: BEACON OF HOPE
GARRO: END OF DAYS

Winter Series- Fantasy Trilogy Books
WINTER'S COMING
WINTER'S HUNT
WINTER'S REVENGE
WINTER'S DISSENSION

Miscellaneous:
RETURN
FREEDOM
SALVATION
Reflection of Mount Flame
The Masked One
The Great Deer

Ingram Content Group UK Ltd.
Milton Keynes UK
UKHW020700240723
425668UK00014B/632